DANCE SISTERS

ALAN CLAY

Virtual Dreams

There was a roar of anger from the crowd, as the police baton-charged down the steps of the Opera House. They were pelted with cans of beer and other missiles, while helicopters buzzed overhead, spotlighting the troublemakers.

Eva felt a gnawing fear in the pit of her stomach. She stood transfixed at the side of the outdoor stage, facing the confrontation on the steps. A truck with a water-cannon mounted on top, drew up to one side.

For some reason, Pearl and Moana were already out there, without her. Pearl was pounding out the energy with her feet, as she always did. And, every now and again, Moana would join her in a sequence of steps, however their voices sounded thin and hollow in the chaotic atmosphere.

Pearl was wearing her trademark T-shirt and pair of faded jeans, while Moana, her mop of fuzzy black hair bouncing as she moved, wore a checked bush-shirt, which flapped about her thighs in a spunky manner.

Eva caught her reflection in a mirror at the side of the stage. Her cropped blond hair, and small chest poking cheekily through her half open shirt, made her look younger than her 24 years, however her face had a timeless sense of helplessness in the face of this crisis of human nature.

Neither Pearl nor Moana seemed disturbed by her absence from stage, which seemed odd, and Eva allowed herself to agonise for a moment over whether to join them. It seemed madness to perform under these conditions.

She watched the sound technicians trying to stop a group of people climbing up the scaffolding of the sound towers, with absolutely no success.

Finally she stepped onto stage, her sense of sisterhood overcoming her fear of the chaos, just as a hail of cans and stones were thrown randomly about by the group who had climbed onto the sound towers.

Then, to the visible horror of the technicians, the cops turned their water-cannon onto the sound towers, and drenched the stage in the process.

There were sparks from some of the equipment, and Pearl was almost swept of her feet. She stood unsteadily for a moment, then turned towards Eva, her T-shirt clinging to her chest, and they caught one another's eye.

"Let's get out of here," Pearl said.

Moana nodded her agreement, and they all leapt off the back of the stage. Eva paused for a moment to shelter under a tarpaulin. The beat of the water from the cannon, sounded on the stage above her, and there was a popping sound like gunfire, and then some screams.

This was followed by a sudden lull, and she decided to make a run for it. She crept out from her hiding place, paused for a moment, to see if she could see the others, then quietly slipped through the backstage area, away from the developing riot.

She found herself out on the street, dodging through the traffic. She couldn't believe this was really happening. A tank rolled to a stop on the promenade leading toward Circular Quay, its engine revving. There were sounds of shattering glass, rattling sounds which were definitely gunfire, and screams.

Panic rippled physically through the people around her, and in a moment they were all moving for cover. Eva allowed herself to be carried along by the flow, up toward Hyde Park.

A news-stand billboard caught her attention. 'Rumours of a COUP!' it declared. Faces, wrenched with emotion, scrambled in all directions.

Eva tried to collect her wits as she ran, found herself to be surprisingly calm, and marvelled, for a time, at how unaffected by the crisis she appeared.

Then two mortar shells slammed into a building in front of her, leaving a gapping hole exposing the innards of the building, and showering rubble onto the people below. And the sound of their screams cut through her illusion of calmness, and she realised how much in shock she must really be.

She desperately wanted to pinch herself and wake up. And because she found that she couldn't, all her years of learning how to deal with the world seemed to flake away like peeling paint. All her experience seemed to mean nothing in the face of this experience, and the horror of it echoed through her desperate pants for breath.

Hyde Park was bristling with troops and tanks, and the river of fleeing people continued on down William Street, and up to the Cross, and Eva allowed herself to be swept along with the flow.

After a while she became almost numb to the crush of people about her, aware only of the physical demands of her body, as she negotiated the abandoned cars and the other flotsam in the river of fleeing people. Her throat felt dry, and the air seemed to rasp the skin as it pumped in and out. The muscles in her thighs began aching from the unaccustomed effort, and finally she felt she had to pause and catch her breath.

Somehow she had reached Kings Cross, and she

found a quiet corner at the entrance to a bank, and lent against the glass window. Her chest was rising and falling violently with the effort to gasp enough breath, and it was some moments before her breathing settled sufficiently for her to take in the environment about her.

The first thing that struck her was the hustlers still sitting at the door to the strip-joint beside her, calling their wares to the stream of passers by.

"Want to see a show?"

"Five dollars! Five dollars!"

"Sexy girls! Lesbian acts!"

Somehow the banality of it only added to the sense of crisis however, and in the next moment several people were carried past on stretchers. One, with his leg blown off, was screaming and dripping a trail of blood. It made no sense to Eva, and she found her mind detaching itself from the chaotic events about her. The torrent of frightened humanity continued to pour past, but she felt somehow removed from its clutches. She felt the sensation physically, as a lightness infusing her body.

For some reason this release brought her suddenly back to the terrifying memory of father's death. She recalled looking down into his grave, and seeing the coffin strewn with flowers and bits of dirt. Then looking at a fragile flower in her hand. And, as she threw the bloom into the grave, she had a crushing sense of vulnerability. And then the flower hit the coffin and lay dead like her father, and she started crying. She had been crying for herself really, she realised, not for her father. Crying for the chaos of everything.

She became aware of voices, and, opening her eyes, found herself lying on a padded bench in a small room. She had that strange sense of waking, yet not remembering where she was, and she lay still, waiting for the memory to come back, and listening to the murmur of voices and clink of cutlery coming from beyond the curtain at one end of the room.

She discovered that her hands were resting in moulded terminals on either side of the bench, and the sight of these awakened a sense of recognition, but she was still unable to recall exactly what they were.

Perhaps she was in a hospital, she thought, as she prised her fingers loose from the spongy layer on the inside of each finger groove, and sat up.

It was two steps to the curtain and, peering through into the hall beyond, she discovered a large video display covering the entire opposite wall, with maybe a hundred people eating at tables before it.

An image of the ancient site of Stonehenge covered the display, and the giant stones set in the windswept English countryside made the figures at the tables seem small and helpless. Eva felt the power of the stones

8

sitting somewhat incongruously, however, in this Australian setting.

The three other walls of the hall, not covered by the display, were lined with curtained cubicles, giving it the feeling of a public bath house. There were no windows, so it was hard to tell what time of day it was.

In front of the video display an intense-looking woman in her thirties dominated a raised table, around which an animated group of people was gathered.

To one side of the display, a familiar looking young man sat in front of some technical equipment, and the sight of him finally triggered something in her memory.

She studied him for further clues. He had the slightly shaggy hair and unkempt appearance of many technicians she knew, however with the chest and bearing of a male model.

Possibly sensing her attention, he looked up, and his eyes seemed to find hers, across the hall. He smiled and, despite her confusion, she enjoyed the contact and smiled back.

Then something clicked, and she recalled him briefing her on the virtual-dream equipment, last night. She turned and looked back at the moulded hand terminals on the bench, and knew that the horror of the riot, and the civil unrest which was still so fresh in her memory, had been an experience generated only for her, and that Sydney was still unspoilt outside.

And, although this realisation was in one sense comforting, she felt an intense anger rising inside her at the trauma it had generated in her.

She pushed herself off from the door post, and crossed to a spare seat at a nearby table, where the smell of fresh coffee was wafting from the open lid of a thermos jug. There were plates of toast, and bowls of cereal. It was breakfast. She sat down.

She poured some coffee, and took a quick gulp. It was hot and strong, and the taste was comforting. However she wished she hadn't let Pearl talk her into trying the virtual experience, and she found her eyes searching the room for her friend, but without success.

"... not long now before the Pluto Probes arrive," she caught a snatch of conversation from the person next to her.

The speaker motioned to the video display, and Eva's attention was caught by a data-box at the top, which was headed 'Pluto Probes', and under which a series of figures were ticking relentlessly over.

She found herself counting the number of digits from the left to work out the number. It was reading over four billion kilometres, she worked out, a distance so huge that it meant nothing to her.

Then the chatter in the room subsided, and she realised that the intense woman at the front table was standing. She must be the leader, Eva thought, as she recalled Pearl talking about the structure of the group. The leader's eyes had a hypnotic gaze, but her face seemed devoid of emotions. She looked at the room in silence for some moments, then held someone at a nearby table mesmerised with a fixed gaze.

"How was it last night?" she asked, and Eva shuddered at the control in her voice, and then squealed with delight as the person who stood up, turned out to be Pearl. A huge sense of relief flooded over her at the sight of her friend.

Drawn by the squeal, Pearl's eyes found hers, and she smiled, if somewhat thinly. She had won her nick name because of the hard glossy front she always presented to the world, but Eva knew the soft woman inside. Seldom was this tender side exposed however, and so she was surprised as the colour now seemed to be rising in Pearl's face.

"It was good," Pearl answered the leader quietly.

Eva remembered her talking of the virtual experiences she'd had in the dream-group, and recalled how exotic it had sounded. "Better than real life," she had said, yet with the confusion of her first dream still very fresh in her nerve ends, Eva felt the strong taste of disappointment in her mouth, and she took another sip of coffee.

"Matt," the leader called to the technician. "Could you tell us the parameters of the dream?" And Eva watched him punch the keys in the desk before him, to call up the information.

There was an awkward pause, and Pearl started to squirm. "I was a lead dancer with the Australian Dance Theatre," she volunteered. "I danced magnificently, and received a standing ovation and awards."

"And was seduced by a teenage groupie," Matt added, his voice ringing quietly through the room. Eva savoured his broad Australian twang, with a hint of a slight southern European accent.

Pearl's face darkened at his revelation. She moved nervously from foot to foot. She wasn't the sort of person who enjoyed sharing her intimate sexual experiences.

Eva felt a growing resentment at the pressure being applied to her friend.

"Anything to share with us about it?" The leader was studying Pearl, enjoying her embarrassment at the attention.

"Not really," Pearl responded.

The leader continued to look at her.

"How was your night?" Pearl cheekily reversed the question.

The leader smiled at her daring, and Eva sensed a competitive respect between them. "Great, as it happens." She looked at a guy sitting at the table beside her, who grinned broadly. "I played the shy virgin, and was well and truly ravished."

A frozen grin sat on Pearl's face, the product of the leader accepting her challenge, and the added pressure this then gave for her to reveal her own secrets.

For an anxious moment there were no words spoken, however the leader then seemed to soften, and she motioned Pearl back to her seat, and gestured to the visual of the big stones behind her.

"What is it?" she asked.

There was another awkward silence, during which her eyes swept the upturned faces, stopping now and again to pin someone mercilessly in their chair. Eva found her heart was beating loudly.

"A place for rituals," someone finally suggested.

"Rituals," she repeated slowly. "What sort?"

"Sacrifices," someone else suggested.

"Fertility rites," a third offered.

She jeered at them with each suggestion. There was an anxious silence about the tables. Then she turned to Matt. "Could you call up the details of the building of Stonehenge?" she asked.

He started punching some keys, and the display behind them flashed through diagrams of the development of the monument from the first earth mounds, to the erection of the big stones.

"Archaeological information suggests that three successive races of people took three hundred years to build what we now call Stonehenge," the leader told them. Again the figures seemed to float past without registering in Eva's confused map of reality. How was such concentrated effort possible amongst such primitive people, she found herself wondering.

"The stones weighed over 5 tons each, and had to be transported up to 240 miles," the leader continued.

Matt keyed a map up on the video, with diagrams of giant stones being slid on planks, and floated on rafts. There were gasps of appreciation from some of the group.

It was certainly awe inspiring, however it seemed somewhat remote from her personal experience, and after a while she found herself watching Matt instead, as he punched the keys to call up the data. Eventually he caught her eye again and winked, and, despite the turmoil of her feelings, she again smiled back.

"The construction work probably took a greater proportion of social resources in the years it was being built, than the Pluto probes have taken today." The leader let the silence punctuate their thoughts, and Eva made a mental note to ask Pearl about the probes. "And for very similar reasons," the leader added.

A series of pictures moved across the display, mostly night shots of stars lining up with the stones, and some of an eclipse, and suddenly Eva recognised the monument for an observatory.

"Three successive races of people over three hundred

years," the leader repeated. Whole generations had laboured to erect the stones, and then been washed away. Eva shook her head at the enormity of the project, and it's seeming futility. They sat in silence for some moments.

"How old is it?" the leader asked.

A hand shot up from a table near the front. "Four thousand years."

"Have we got anything like this in Australia?" she asked.

There was silence in the studio.

"Any archaeological sites comparable in age or scope?" she asked.

Again there was silence, and it seemed to build until it could only be broken by a scream, and suddenly Eva recalled something from school.

"Isn't there something similar in Western Australia which is much older?" she called out.

The leader continued to look about the faces in the room without responding, so Eva was left uncertain whether her contribution had been heard.

"It takes an absolute newcomer to the breakfast table," the leader said slowly, surprising Eva by her knowledge of who she was, "to shed light on this question for us." She motioned to Matt, and the visual changed to a remote outcrop, rising out of the tropical woodlands of the Kimberley ranges, which was dotted with enormous sculptured boulders. The visual zoomed in, and detailed circular engravings, faded and weathered by many years, could be seen on the outcrop.

"And, of course, much older," the leader agreed. "how much older would you guess?" she challenged someone at her table.

"Twice as old," he ventured bravely, for he obviously had no idea.

"And you?" The leader turned to someone else.

"Ten times as old," she suggested, again obviously guessing.

Eva was thankful that the question wasn't being put to her, however the mystery of it had engaged her interest, and the rest of her coffee was left untouched before her.

"Twice as much again," the leader told them. "It was created around 75,000 years ago." She let the figure hang in the air, and they clinked, and slurped, and chewed their way around the number for a while. "75,000" she repeated.

Eva felt at once proud of this ancient heritage, as an Australian, and at the same time somewhat alienated from it, by her European ancestry.

Someone entered the studio, and, through the open door, the sound of a siren found its way up the stairs from amid the traffic noise of Kings Cross. The newcomer crossed to Pearl's table, and Eva watched him whisper something in her ear, to which she nodded.

"So when we look at our involvement with the probes," the leader continued, "we also have to understand that the research has been going on for that length of time, and not expect any quick results."

Eva felt someone touch her on the shoulder, and she jumped in surprise. It was Pearl.

"Angel's left a message that she needs to see us straight away," she whispered. "You'd better get your stuff."

Eva gulped some more coffee, and looked about at the array of cubicles. It had been very dark last night when she arrived. "Which was mine?" she asked, and Pearl pointed towards the back corner of the studio.

2
Sisters

Eva stood in the doorway, and put on her sunglasses. Kings Cross had a somewhat grainy feel this morning. As if she'd got up too early, she thought. Behind her, in the hall, leaflets on a notice-board stirred in the breeze, and she let the random sounds sift through her thoughts as she waited.

Finally Pearl came running down the stairs, two at a time, and they walked off towards the underground. The morning was already hot, and Eva felt the weather reflected in a heaviness in the pit of her stomach.

They passed a one-legged man, sitting on a battered dustbin with a bucket of red tulips in front of him. The blooms stood proud and fresh against the grime of the pavement. "Want'ta buy a flower?" he called.

Pearl stopped to buy one, which surprised Eva. It

wasn't like her, and she was even more surprised when Pearl turned and offered her the bloom. Eva kissed her, on the cheek, and saw her flush slightly.

"I didn't go for the virtual dream stuff," she told Pearl, feeling the need to confide the unease in her stomach.

"What happened?"

Eva tried to explain what she remembered. The images seemed to tumble out in a chaotic fashion, and she knew she had only partial success, but Pearl still just nodded.

"That's standard," she said. "They say you first have to dissolve your reality framework, so that you can make maximum use of the potential of the virtual system."

The words chased one another along the street. What did they mean? Eva wondered. "Is that what happens to everyone?" she asked.

Pearl shook her head. "No, you direct the experience to some extent... but mine was quite similar." She shook her head at the memory. "I had the audience attack me with tomatoes."

Eva couldn't help but smile. She knew how Pearl felt just before a show, the audience out there waiting. "But what is it doing to us, to have these experiences?" she asked.

"It's all about letting go of who we are, so that we can grow into someone new," Pearl told her.

They fell silent, and the rhythm of their footsteps

beat out the waiting moments.

"Anyway, it's really just like watching television," Pearl said.

Eva flashed back to the horror of the civil unrest experience, and for a moment the buildings on either side of the street seemed to crumble. She shook her head. "It feels more real. It must have more effect. Besides, I choose what I watch on television."

Pearl nodded. "You get to control the dream too, later on."

Eva felt uneasy with the way she threw off the answer. She was usually more sceptical.

"It does get better," Pearl assured her, with a small smile.

"It would have to," Eva told her. "I can't believe they actually charge for it."

"You didn't pay for last night, did you?"

Eva shook her head. "I did the free introductory one, because you invited me." They pounded the pavement in silence for some more moments. Eva still felt a gnawing doubt crawling around in her guts. "Why did she put you on the spot like that at breakfast?" she asked.

"The line is, that you have to share your virtual experiences, so you realise them for the illusions they are, otherwise it's like masturbation."

Again they walked in silence. Pearl started playing with the rhythm of her footsteps, and, as Eva found herself dancing to keep up, her mind moved on to other things.

"What's the story with those Pluto probes?" she asked.

Pearl shrugged. "Some space mission the group's involved with." She grinned. "Pretty crazy huh? The feed comes direct from the probes, and is decoded by the group."

"Across 4 billion kilometres?" Eva asked, the figure winking at her in her mind.

Pearl nodded. "Something like that."

Eva found she still couldn't get her head around it. She watched her friend's feet arrange themselves amidst the cracks in the pavement as she danced along beside her. Pearl was like her big sister, she thought.

Angel smiled as they entered, her eyes lightly greeting each of them in turn. She had a poise about her movements, and was dressed formally in a suit. Eva suspected that she dressed that way to belie her youth, for, without it, she had something of the feel of a young upstart. She motioned them to sit down, and her eyes returned to something she was typing into the laptop on her desk.

Moana was sitting by the window. She was wearing a white singlet, which clung to her chest, accentuating the flavour of her brown skin. On her shoulder rippled a delicate tattoo of a fern leaf, and behind her mop of frizzy black hair the office window looked out from the 41st floor onto Sydney harbour. It was a stunning day.

Pearl sat without hesitation in the seat furthest away from Moana, leaving Eva to sit reluctantly between them.

Moana grinned, and clapped her on the thigh. "You guys didn't come home last night, eh?" she teased them. "I had the whole house to myself."

Eva pulled her hand off. She felt too vulnerable for Moana's sexual camaraderie. That's why she wasn't in a relationship at the moment herself.

"Ain't your business any more," Pearl said coldly, and the tone of her voice seemed to reach down into a deep well of emotion.

Moana grinned brazenly back at her, and then turned to Angel. "Which reminds me, you said you'd take me out to dinner. Maybe you could take me to the Mardigras Party."

"I don't know if I like you that much," Angel told her, looking up from the laptop with a small smile.

Was there something going on between them? Eva wondered fleetingly.

"It's also the same night as the Song Awards." The boss finished typing, and inserted some sheets of paper into the printer, her clean movements demonstrating a comforting precision and efficiency. Pearl was also

22

watching her, and Eva was relieved to discover her street-wise scepticism showing in every muscle. Angel brought it out in her.

Eva's eyes drifted back to the window. She savoured the familiar outline of Moana's hair, against the timeless features of the Harbour Bridge and the criss-crossing wakes of the yachts. The printer hummed in the background, and she felt her muscles relax back into the chair. It was leather. Very comfortable.

Then there was a bark from the phone, and for a moment the image of the harbour felt like it might shatter and fall away into emptiness behind Moana's familiar features. Then Angel picked up the receiver, and passed Moana a printout with the other hand.

For some reason Eva recalled the feed from the probes on the video display. "This Pluto business is spooky, isn't it?" she found herself saying.

Moana looked up from the sheet of paper. "What Pluto business?" The harbour stood intact behind her.

"The probes," Eva told her. Moana looked at her blankly. She hadn't heard of it, Eva realised, and the reality jolted her back to the meeting. Angel was clinching some deal on the phone, and she passed Eva a copy of the printout, and gave one to Pearl. It was a press release.

"Dance Sisters to enter Australasian Song Awards," Eva read. "The Dance Sisters have enjoyed phenomenal success over the last six months, since the expansion of the duo to a trio, with the addition of Eva Jones to the line-up."

"That's a bit steep, about Eva, isn't it?" Pearl couldn't help but ask, and Eva poked her in the ribs. She was still having to prove herself to Pearl, much of the time.

Angel put the phone down. "We can still change anything in the press release," she told them.

"It's fine," Moana said, handing back her copy.

Angel motioned her to keep it, and, picking up a pile of booklets, handed them each one. "This is the recording agreement," she explained. "Assigning the rights from the Awards, and outlining the promotional requirements on the winners."

Eva felt her eyes widen as she leafed through the pages of the contract.

"Take them away and read them," Angel suggested. "As long as they're signed by the press conference tomorrow, we'll be okay."

Eva sat on a speaker cabinet, and swung her legs so they beat a rhythm on the vinyl clad material on the side. It made her feel like a little girl again. She savoured the excitement of the rehearsal room. The shiny lines of the microphone stands and the crisp texture of the sound-proofing on the walls spoke to her of adventure and success. After months of slogging around the pub circuit, they were about to make it. She could feel it looming over them.

Pearl opened the door, and stood talking with Moana in the doorway. They were conferring in their serious, sisterly way, that they could effect one day, and still be shouting at one another the next.

Eva couldn't hope to develop the intimacy with either of them that they had with each other, she thought. She drummed her heels against the case, and watched the flash of communication between them; the small twists and turns of their heads, the contact of the eyes. Pearl was on the defensive about something, she realised.

Her fingers found her pack of tarot cards in the pocket of her jacket, and, taking them out, she unwrapped them.

The door slammed, and Pearl came over to stand beside her.

"You should come to the lecture tonight," she said,

"Why?"

"It's the Pluto mission."

Eva found she didn't want to go. "Maybe I will," she said, and she started to shuffle the cards.

Moana burst back into the room, and strode over to them, the bounce of her hair accentuating the playfulness of her movements. "The techie's on his way," she announced.

Pearl was lying on the floor fiddling with a radio microphone, and she made a show of looking at her watch, and rolling her eyes.

Eva drummed her feet against the speaker again. She was wary of taking sides between them

Moana's eye caught the spread of tarot cards, and Eva saw a look of mistrust cross her face. Although she was still trying to understand the reading herself, she picked them up and wrapped them again, in deference to her friend. She had expected a reading about the success of their participation in the Awards, but there seemed to be several unsettling influences, which she couldn't decipher.

"So, you were on the hunt again last night?" Moana probed Pearl.

Pearl looked at Eva, and raised her eyebrows in exasperation. Despite her misgivings about the dream-group, Eva felt pleased to be part of her inner club.

"Those days are over," Pearl told Moana.

"At that group, was it?" The distrust was evident in Moana's voice.

"Come and have a look," Pearl told her.

Moana chuckled at the idea, but Eva felt the raw nerves of her split with Pearl just below the surface of her attitude.

"Really," Pearl pursued her, "come and see for yourself, if you really want to know what you're talking about."

Suddenly the daggers were out, and it was Moana's turn to look to Eva for support.

Eva felt awash with emotions however, unable to take a position in relation to either of her friends. "I think it's important that we try and understand one another, if we're going to continue working together," she found herself saying. "I think it's worth coming to one of the evening sessions, so that you can see what Pearl's into," she told Moana.

"I'll go, if Pearl signs the Awards contract," Moana declared. It seemed too good to be true, and Eva turned to Pearl with a look of triumph, and then realised from her expression that it wasn't that simple.

"I've got some questions about the contract," Pearl admitted, "with the recording rights, and the commitment of time, if we win." And Eva suddenly understood both the interaction in the doorway, and the unsettling influences in the tarot spread.

A technician burst into the studio, and dropped a pile of leads on the floor. He looked over to them, and Moana give him a lazy wave.

The technician motioned to Pearl to try blowing into the

microphone, but there was no response from the equipment, and the image of her lips soundlessly caressing the black sponge head looked somehow comical.

Eva watching the parade of images, as the technician checked the leads to the sound desk. What was the difference between this experience, and the virtual ones? she wondered. They both felt as real at the time, but there were lasting consequences in this reality, she realised, and comic book immortality in the virtual system. The speaker beneath her burst suddenly into life, and Pearl's voice bounced about the room.

After just a few minutes they were warmed up and their voices began to dance with one another. It didn't matter what personal space they were in, they always seemed to achieve a delicate harmony in their work. It was a measure of their professionalism, and Eva took heart from this.

As she sang, she felt her muscles relaxing and her voice vibrate through her body. She sensed the support of Pearl's energy, and the drama of Moana's. She heard her own voice play amongst the others, sometimes reaching a vibrant synthesis, sometimes counter-pointing. They each had a good voice, but together their voices had a life which was unbelievably powerful.

3 *Cosmic Perspective*

Tonight the tables had disappeared from the room where Eva had found herself at breakfast this morning, and the chairs were now arranged in a large horseshoe, with the video display at the open end. A panorama of the night sky was spread lavishly across it. There must have been several hundred people in the room, and although Moana had made a point of requesting that they sit together, the introductory dancing left them in different parts of the room, as the lights dimmed and the lecture began.

Eva found a seat, and allowed her breathing to slowly return to normal.

"The Pluto encounter which we will witness in the coming weeks will be the first time humanity will have the chance of seeing this, furthest known planet of our solar system, close up," the leader informed them. She was standing in a spotlight, at a lectern in front of the video screen. "Which is not to say that the planet has not been studied meticulously since it was first discovered earlier this century, because it has."

The video screen flashed through hazy photographic images, which must have been taken through the Hubble telescope. They showed ragged polar ice caps, and clusters of mysterious bright and dark features on the surface of the planet.

Matt was on the controls again. His body was alert, like an animal sniffing the wind, his total focus on the leader. He seemed so alive, so enjoying his role, and embracing each new experience, that Eva found it refreshing just to watch him.

"One of the mysteries which we hope will be revealed, is that Pluto appears to be a very small planet," the leader continued, "and yet its influence on the orbits of other planets in the solar system should make it heavier." The enthusiasm in her voice was infectious, and Eva felt her interest aroused by the mystique of the planet. "We know that Pluto has an elliptical orbit, much longer and flatter than any of the other planets. And that at times it passes inside the orbit of Neptune, and ceases to be the outermost planet in the solar system."

Behind her the video threw up a diagram of the concentric orbits of the planets.

Eva found her eye caught by a woman who was

moving restlessly in her seat on the other side of the horseshoe of seats. She was young and pretty, but was wearing an old fashioned dress patterned with prints of flowers which looked cheaply made, and sat awkwardly on her thin shoulders. Behind her, two men were standing guard on either side of the door out into the hall, their arms folded across their chests.

"We've just come through such a period when Pluto was closer than Neptune," the leader told them. "Astrology tells us that should have been a time of great upheaval and changes in the world, and we can see these changes in the events of recent years, both here in Australia, and overseas."

"But what about God?" the young woman in the flower dress suddenly interjected, and there was a ripple of laughter from around the circle of chairs.

The leader ignored her. "Pluto in astrological terms represents the process of transformation," she told them. "It's the making of something new out of something old, which is the stuff of life at every level. It also represents the unconscious, and its discovery is said to represent humanities growing awareness of the process of transformation in our lives."

Suddenly the woman who had interjected stood up, knocking her chair over in the process. She was moving in a jerky, uncoordinated way as she turned to the door. Then she stopped, and stood staring at the guards, uncertain what to do next. Eva couldn't decide whether to feel sorry for her, or frightened of her, because she seemed so weird.

The leader was clearly irritated, and she signalled to the guards to restrain the interjector, while she strode over to deal with the problem. The guards grabbed her by an arm each, and held her so firmly that they almost lifted her off the floor, which was totally unnecessary, as she had gone limp at their first touch.

Beside the door hung a fire-extinguisher and the leader grabbed it, as she strode up. There was such a force in the gesture that Eva felt afraid the leader would throw it at the woman, but instead she hit the trigger and hosed the woman down with the dry foam mist. Her unexpected behaviour sent Eva into shock. It affected the weird woman the same way.

The leader motioned to the guards to escort the woman back to her seat, and she walked back to the lectern. Eva realised that there had been a bass note from a synthesiser providing a sound effect to the action, and this rose gently in tone and then disappeared.

"For the old astrologers the solar system ended with Saturn," the leader said, resuming her position at the lectern, and continuing as if nothing had occurred.

The lights in the room dimmed, the video energised again, and an image of Saturn leapt onto the screen. Eva was drawn out of her sense of shock by the splendour of the rings around the planet.

"For thousands of years Saturn was the end of the solar system, the limit of our known reality," the leader told them. "And suddenly Uranus was discovered."

The video image sped away from Saturn, and fixed on a point of light which quickly grew into a planet with what appeared to be a hazy atmosphere. It also had a couple of rings, and seemed to be spinning on its side, instead of up and down.

"Since its discovery in 1781, Uranus has broken through the old limits with flashes of insight, lateral ideas, and a more intuitive perspective." The leader's voice was hypnotic in quality.

The image on the video moved on, and the speed and clarity of the move made it feel like the room, and everyone in it, was being sucked out into the universe. Eva clutched instinctively to her seat. After a short time the image fixed on a planet which grew until it was too large to fill the screen. It was a swirling blue-green planet, and she could see what looked like huge storms in the swirling cloud patterns.

"The discovery of Neptune in 1846 represented humanities search for new, more encompassing, visions of ourselves and our place in the scheme of things. The old mythologies can no longer deal with the individual spiritual nature being awakened slowly in each of us."

The video panned away from Neptune, out beyond

the moons which represented the furthest point of human exploration to date, and the promise of Pluto loomed somewhere tantalisingly in the darkness.

The weird woman was drawing attention to herself again by moving restlessly in her seat, and Eva spotted Moana sitting six or seven seats away from her. It would have been hard to tell in the half-light if it really was her friend, except that her frizzy hair was pretty distinctive.

"As each planet was discovered, so its energies have been awakened in the human psyche," the leader told them. "And now it's Pluto's turn. The planet which was discovered as recently as 1930, and represents our power to make or break our reality in a very finite way. The enormous power inherent in physical reality which is forming our world constantly as we speak."

Again, Eva felt herself clutching her seat.

"Over the next few weeks as the information from the probes comes in, humanity will have its first chance to explore this planet, and, as always, we'll be leading the way here in the Group, and learning from this information." Eva felt a surge of emotion. "And that concludes tonight's lecture," the leader told them, and she bowed slightly, to polite applause.

The lights came back up, and there was a loud snort from the young woman who had interjected earlier. She bent forward to cradle her head in her hands, and started moaning quietly.

"I probably don't need to remind anyone," the leader said, pacing into the centre of the horseshoe of chairs, "that there's a lot of research material available in our library, if any of you want to pursue these issues further."

She was slowly approaching the woman as she spoke, and as she passed Moana, Eva was caught by her friend's expression. Her face had a cat-like intensity, staring fixedly at the leader. Something in this look awoke Eva out of the trance of the experience, and her eyes panned around the circle in search of Pearl. She was sitting near the front of the room, with a look of radiance in her face, like an aura.

The leader cleared her throat. She was standing right in front of the woman, directly in her line of vision, daring her to respond, but the woman just stared with a belligerent look, and moaned quietly.

For an eternity they stayed like that, caught in a power struggle, the idiot and the leader, both certain that they could beat the other. However unfortunately the idiot's strength was based only on innocence, and this was shattered as the leader suddenly started roaring abuse at her.

Eva's heart leapt to her throat, and she saw Moana's expression also break with a look of shocked surprise. She felt thankful that, from where she was sitting, Moana wouldn't be able to see the look of sheer terror which appeared on the young woman's face. This wasn't the introduction to the group that Eva had envisaged for her friend.

Not content with this however, the leader stepped toward the woman, grabbed her by the front of her skirt, and dragged her into the middle of the circle of seats.

Eva moved uncomfortably to the edge of her seat. Although this behaviour seemed incredible, it felt impossible to challenge due to the empowering acceptance of the horseshoe of faces.

Realising what a mistake she had made in challenging the giant, the crazy one started blabbering something unintelligible.

The leader dropped her in a heap on the floor. "Do I come over to your place and disturb your evening?" she asked rhetorically, for there was little chance of a sensible reply.

Suddenly it was too much for Moana, and she leapt to her feet, and strode to the woman's side. For a long moment she stood eyeballing the leader, taking her measure in her no-nonsense way. And then, taking the woman by the elbow, Moana helped her to her feet.

Eva wanted to cry out to her not to interfere, but she knew you couldn't tell Moana that, and secretly she admired her stand.

However the leader simply stood and watched as Moana led the woman towards the door. She let them almost get there, before, with the merest nod of her head, motioning to the guards on either side of the door, and they moved to block any exit.

Moana stopped, and for another long moment there was a stand-off.

The leader was demonstrating her power. "The crazy one can go," she said, and the security line parted. Slowly the woman detached herself from Moana, and was almost sucked out through the door.

Moana turned back to face the room. Thankfully the leader seemed satisfied to have demonstrated her control, and she was now pacing back towards the lectern. Moana glanced behind her at the line of guards still standing in front of the door, and then with a hint of swagger, she walked back to her seat.

Eva breathed a sigh of relief that she had been allowed to challenge the leader's authority in this way, and get away with it. And yet, as her friend sat down, she couldn't help but feel that the leader had strengthened her position, by being able to accept such defiance, and then to co-opt its energy to rid the gathering of the crazy woman.

"That was a brave and compassionate action by our Kiwi friend," the leader encouraged Moana, further confusing Eva's frame of reference for the experience.

She caught sight of Pearl for the first time since the drama began. She was clearly challenged by Moana's audacity in standing up to the leader, and it had triggered some deep competitive emotions. Her body was quivering in the chair.

Matt whispered something in the leader's ear.

"I understand this Kiwi in shining armour is a friend of yours," the leader told Pearl.

Pearl looked awkwardly about the circle, uncertain where to let her eyes rest, the street-wise cool suddenly out of depth.

"In fact this is your former lover, who you have told us so much about," the leader confronted her.

Now all the eyes in the room turned to re-evaluate Moana. She glared back at them, and Eva's heart fell. This was not the way to get Moana on side, she knew.

The leader leaned toward Matt, and asked him something to which, at first, he seemed reluctant to respond. Then he nodded, and pointed towards Eva.

"And I believe the third member of the trio is also here tonight," the leader announced, and Eva felt the eyes probing her out.

She cursed Matt, under her breath. Then half stood, and nodded her head in greeting, to end the excruciating experience as soon as possible. However, immediately the leader's eyes fixed on her, there was such energy in her look that Eva felt blessed with the contact, and she lost her feeling of self consciousness.

"We must have a small performance, now that you

are all here," the leader told them, and she looked from Eva, to Moana, and back to Pearl.

Pearl had an aroused look on her face, and without a hesitation she leapt to her feet and strode into the centre of the circle. Moana also rose to the challenge, she obviously felt confident now, and she looked powerful as she walked towards Pearl.

The pressure of the eyes was too strong to refuse, and Eva also rose to her feet, and walked over to meet the others.

As she reached them, they broke into what they hoped would soon be their new hit, 'Dangerous Times'. They had sung it so many times, that it just flowed.

She watched Moana's face as they sang, and saw her expression slowly soften. Eva hadn't given any thought to the song, it had just been the first one in her mind. It was only later, as Moana launched with particular gusto into the verse about "Gurus on every corner, suckers for the answer", that she realised the relevance of the lyrics.

She felt their voices resound throughout the room, somehow settling the energy of the gathering with the melody and the harmony. She began to enjoy herself. Their music was once again triumphing and bringing people together.

As they finished the leader led the gathering in resounding applause, which seemed to make everything all right again. However, throughout her life Eva was to retain an image of those encircling faces, open in their rapture, yet, by their encirclement, somehow menacing in nature.

"I think we can only offer free Dreams in gratitude, to each of them," the leader declared, in response to further applause.

Eva felt something catch in her throat at her suggestion. She glanced at Pearl, who gave her a warm smile, part thanks, part encouragement. Then she looked at Moana, who was still looking defiant.

"What's this 'dreams' she's on about?" Moana asked.

"Virtual dreams, you know?" Eva prompted her.

Moana snorted in a way which expressed her contempt at the suggestion. She was so real, Eva impulsively kissed her on the cheek. It was the first time she had kissed Moana, and she felt her soften at the touch.

Then everyone seemed to stand, as if at some unseen signal, and many of the crowd pressed forward to congratulate the three of them. Several wanted to shake Eva's hand. She felt at once flattered, and a little startled at the turn of events.

Matt pushed through the crowd and stood in front of her. His eyes were sparkling. "You were fantastic," he told her.

There was a wash of music about them, and people started to dance. She felt ensnared in his rapture. They were staring at one another so intimately, that she felt sure her secret feelings were all on display, and she didn't know what to say.

Instead she reached up and caressed his cheek lightly with her fingers, and, feeling his skin warm to her touch, ran her hand behind his neck and squeezed the muscles gently. They were firm and yet yielded to her grip. She felt his hand caressing her thigh, and then her buttock. Her muscles thrilled to the sudden intimacy of their contact. Then, glancing around, she noticed that they were the only people not dancing, and she pulled back.

"Maybe we can meet sometime," he suggested.

"I'd like that," she surprised herself by responding, as their bodies started picking up the energy from the surrounding dancers.

"I'm here tomorrow afternoon. If you want to drop in."

She nodded, and felt suddenly warm towards this new person in her life.

4

Public Property

"What I don't like is the way they want to parade us around, in the month after the competition," Pearl said. She was rocking slightly from side to side in her chair.

Eva couldn't believe that she was still holding out at this late stage, and the heat of the spotlights on her cheeks fanned the sense of urgency. Beyond them however, the room was strangely empty. All the chairs, the tape-recorders, the microphones, and the cameras, stood ready. The expectant hush was everywhere, but the reporters and camera operators were nowhere to be seen.

"They get to tell us where to go, and what to do," Pearl went on, "so we can't do other work, and then they only cover the expenses."

Moana was sitting curled up in the chair between them, her knees hugged to her chest, and a small smile on her lips at Pearl's procrastination.

Angel shrugged. "That's only if you win," she reminded Pearl gently. She had a way of talking which could convince anyone of anything. "And they're only asking that you do the main TV shows, and a couple of big gala-events."

"It will be great promotion, if we get that far," Eva said. She couldn't understand why Pearl wasn't jumping at the opportunity.

"I'm beginning to wonder whether you really want to," Angel told Pearl. She held her gaze, challenging Pearl to respond, however she made no move to do so.

Eva felt light headed from a restless night's sleep, and she found herself giggling at little things. The childish jut of Pearl's chin now set it off, which unfortunately only made her friend even more determined not to respond.

"You've got to face the reality that you've got a contract with me to manage you," Angel said. "You're not doing it yourself from the back-room any more." This was the issue, Eva realised, and she allowed herself to sink back into the upholstery of the chair in an attempt to avoid the confrontation.

"We have a deal to do some work together," Angel reminded Pearl, and the silky way she said it, made Eva want to believe that everything she touched turned to gold. Sometimes, she knew, Angel over-reached herself, but for the most part she seemed to be able to deliver on her visions.

Still Pearl didn't respond.

"Look I'm not going to come on stage and tell you how to sing," Angel pursued her, "and I don't want you in the office telling me how to book the gigs."

This finally stung Pearl into a response. "But the first thing you did as manager was to question the sound of the act," she spat back at her manager.

Eva felt her position to be suddenly threatened. She recalled Pearl's face during the audition. She hadn't been able to understand it at the time, but now knew what a challenge accepting her had been for Pearl.

"That's why we started working with Angel," Moana jumped in. "You remember?" Despite her relaxed posture, her body now looked coiled ready to pounce. "We'd gone as far as we could, with just the two of us." They eyed one another like cats. One wrong movement, and one of them would pounce.

"What about the recording rights?" Pearl asked her, her body strangely still, but her face quivering with energy. "You think it's fair that we only get a 5% royalty?"

Moana placed her feet on the floor. "You're just scared of winning," she challenged her. "It's your weakness, eh? No real guts. That's why you need that therapy group, where you can have pretend experiences instead." The tattoo of the fern on her shoulder was rippling, as if blowing in the wind. Her motionless gaze held Pearl transfixed.

It felt like the next pounce would finish the confrontation one way or the other, and despite her deep unease at the argument, or perhaps because of it, Eva found herself giggling again.

Angel waved the copies of the agreement. "Come on guys!" There was too much at stake for her to allow this personal stuff to interfere with their plans. "We've gone through too much, to cop out now."

. "Come on Pearl," Eva encouraged her. She really wanted this gig, it meant everything to her, and it felt like they couldn't keep the press waiting much longer. She leaned across Moana and waved a pen under Pearl's nose.

Pearl only looked at it, in studied rejection, and, to her embarrassment, Eva giggled again. Then, to cover her feelings, she took one of the agreements from Angel and resolutely scrawled her own signature on it.

She discovered that her heart was beating with the adrenaline of challenging Pearl's big-sister role in this way, but passed it to Moana, who added her signature.

Pearl made no move to sign however, and her chin became set in a stubborn jut. "Something just feels wrong," she murmured.

"You've had it for 24 hours," Angel told her. "If you

seriously wanted to change anything, you would have been negotiating those changes. This way is unprofessional." There was a pregnant pause. "So either sign it, or we're history."

Eva watched Pearl almost smile, despite herself. It was this hard-nosed approach which she respected, and needed, in their manager. And, under the relentless pressure of all three pairs of eyes, she finally took the pen and signed.

There was a rush of conversation, as Angel opened the doors to the foyer and a flood of people poured into the room, slowly followed by a smell of bodies gathered in a confined space. The television camera-men started checking their equipment, while the reporters gradually assembled behind them.

Their presence made Eva nervous, but she sensed that Angel had everything under control. She was weaving backward and forward between the reporters, smoothing out any feeling of frustration at the delay. This was her medium.

Eva's thoughts returned to Matt. He had also figured somewhere in her dreams last night. Pearl had opened the wound of her participation in the trio, and she sensed that the answer to this behaviour lay with the Dream-group, and Matt was the best person to talk to about it.

Angel coughed to get attention. "Members of the media... I'd like to welcome you to the launch of the Dance Sisters entry into the Australasian Song Awards."

The mumbling in the room gradually subsided.

"You should all have a folder with some brief biographies, the lyrics, and some promotional material. If you don't, come and get one from me later." She paused, and there was only the sound of shuffling feet. "Who wants to go first?"

A woman crouching at the front caught Angel's attention, and then turned to Pearl and Moana. "You've both developed something of a role model status for young women in recent years, haven't you?" she asked, and they smiled.

"Particularly with your forthright statements on women's issues and the environment," she continued, and the smiles grew a little wider. Eva found herself wondering why she was pandering to their egos like this, and so she wasn't really surprised by the next turn in the line of questioning.

"You've also made much of your lesbian relationship in the past, but we haven't heard a lot about this recently. Is that still a vital part of your music?"

Pearl came erect in her seat at the question, and looked directly at the woman. "I know, for many people, our relationship has symbolised the freedom we all have to experiment with our lives despite the conditioning of society," she said, "and naturally this is still an important part of our art."

"But there have been rumours that you've split?" the woman pursued her, and Eva cringed as the line of Pearl's mouth hardened.

"I hope our music transcends our personal relationships," she responded icily. "Which, anyway, I prefer to keep private."

"Isn't it true that you're now involved with that virtual-sex group in Kings Cross?" another woman asked.

Pearl wasn't having a good day. She studied the reporters outline in the gloom for an eternal moment. "You ask that as if it were something weird," she finally said. "We have virtual technology around us all the time; in our games, in our schools and libraries, and through the Internet and Pay TV..."

"But not virtual sex!" someone interrupted her.

"The government itself censors the software and regulates the technology," Pearl shot back. "And, anyway, as I said, I prefer to keep some things private."

"Do you also do that virtual-sex stuff?" another reporter asked Moana.

Moana had been enjoying Pearl's predicament, but now she was forced to her support. "Questions like that is why we've been forced to speak out in the past about our sexuality." She shook her head, and her hair extended the gesture. "We support individual rights and I guess our relationship has symbolised that."

Pearl nodded beside her. "There's no problem with our search elsewhere. We're different people."

"There have been allegations of underage sex, of group sex, of corruption, and of denial of human rights, in this, so-called, 'Dream-group'." Another reporter put to Pearl. "What do you say to those claims?"

"Again, that's either my personal business," Pearl told her, "or if it's an official question to the group you're talking about, then it should be put to them."

"Come on guys," Angel called from the side, irritated by the line of questioning.

"I would just like to say something to finish with this topic," Pearl added. "There are many experiences we can't have in the real world. Perfectly legitimate learning experiences which just aren't possible within the structure of the lives that each of us lead." Her fingers played nervously with one another as she spoke. "Dreaming gives us the opportunity to experience things which we can't explore in our everyday lives." And after a moment she added, "and art also does this." Somehow it didn't quite sound like her own words. "Now that we have virtual reality, we can create experiences which are designed to assist our growth, and these are not less valid, because they are unreal. In the same way that flight simulation, for example, is any less a valid way to train pilots."

What she was saying made sense, but warning bells were flashing somewhere in Eva's mind, and then she recalled their discussion as they walked to Angel's office yesterday morning.

"It's just like watching TV..." she heard Pearl answer her uncertainty, and she found herself wondering which it was; a valid life experience, or just an entertainment?

A man pushed to the front and stepped into the pool of light. Eva found him looking directly at her, and the pace of her heartbeat increased a few notches. "As a new member of the act," he asked, "how have you found fitting into what was such a strong double act?"

Eva experienced herself as floating for a moment, while she weighed up an answer. "This is everything I've dreamed of doing," she told him. "And I have good supportive relationships with both Pearl and Moana." She looked at them, and they nodded.

"It's gone very smoothly," Moana said.

"So your joining the act wasn't the catalyst for their split?" he persisted.

Eva steadied herself, and then all her frustration at their line of questioning came bubbling out. "We sing, we do it very well," she told him. "I think it's generally agreed that my voice has strengthened the sound of the Dance Sisters, and that we now present a more dynamic, full voiced act on stage. And that's what's important.

That's what people want to know. Not some emotional grubbing around."

"Right on!" Angel rushed to her support.

"Obviously we go through different personal spaces just like everyone else," Eva continued. Her nervousness had disappeared, and now she felt empowered by the opportunity of saying how she felt. "We all have relationships, but I'd like to think that we are professional enough to rise above that, and produce an exciting performance no matter what." Both the others were nodding, and Angel gave her the thumbs up. "And I think that's what the fans want to know too," she finished, a little apologetically for her lecturing tone.

There was a pause, and then a wave of laughter rippled through the room. "And they also want to know," Angel added, "that the new single will be first performed tomorrow at a free outdoor concert at Darling Harbour."

There was further laughter.

"Do you agree that Eva's voice has added to the sound of the Dance Sisters?" someone at the back called, it seemed to be directed to Moana.

Moana smiled. "Australia is a big land," she answered somewhat obtusely. "If I can say that as a Kiwi. It's a country which demands a range and a resonance in its music. A full bodied brew. Eva brings new flavour to our art, and I think it somehow makes it more Australian."

Eva's pride swelled at the affirmation. She had grown

up with that first generation cultural tension of making Sydney her home, and yet not really feeling the same as everyone else because her parents retained their native German culture, so it meant a lot to her to be accepted as Australian, even if it was by a former Kiwi.

5

The Files

Eva walked hesitantly up the last few steps. She could hear Matt's voice in the office, and it was only this familiarity that kept her moving forward against her increasing sense of shyness. As she turned the corner, she was acutely aware of the scene, as he sat with two colleagues stuffing what looked like a newsletter into envelopes.

"Hi Eva," he said, as soon as he saw her. He stood, and crossed over to her.

She felt relieved that she didn't have to initiate the contact. "You said you'd be here," she said, rather needlessly.

He nodded, and smiled. They stood looking a one another, and then he stroked her arm, and she felt her body relax. The intensity of his eye contact felt too strong, however, so she turned slightly away, and caught sight of the other two watching them intently.

"Shall we go out and find a cafe?" she suggested.

He looked hesitant, and his colleagues seemed to lean closer.

"I thought I might show you the library," he responded.

Perhaps he wasn't allowed out, she thought. "Sure," she agreed.

He motioned her back through the door, stroked her back as she stepped through, and squeezed her shoulder softly to turn her to the left.

She enjoyed his touch.

The library door closed behind them, and she heard him scratching around on the wall for the light switch, however now that she was actually here, she was less certain that it was the right move. The light came on, and she found herself staring at a row of screens, mounted above a table containing video players and a computer. She had expected books, but only one wall of the room rewarded her expectations.

She sensed a hesitation from him, and wondered if he was also feeling nervous about being alone with her, which seemed strange given his physical forwardness in the office, or if he were maybe wary of what they might discover here.

"How do we get the machines on?" she asked, touching him lightly on the arm to encourage him. "Or are you having second thoughts?" His hesitancy made her feel more comfortable.

By way of answering, he placed a card into a slot beside the light switch, just as he had outside to open the door, and systematically the machines switched themselves on and proceeded with a status check.

"Where do you get the card?" she asked.

"They give you one on initiation."

"What's that?"

"When you commit yourself to the group."

"Have you done that?"

"Obviously," he said, waving the card.

"What does it involve?"

He smiled, and looked at her in a way which seemed to leave more questions than it answered. "You better talk to Pearl about it," he advised, and the tone of his voice signalled to her not to pursue it further.

There were a number of swivel chairs in the room, and he pulled one over to the multimedia table and sat down. "What do you want to see?" he asked.

She had agreed to the library simply to get him away from the others in the office, and so now her mind jumped on the first idea it found. "Let's start with the Pluto probes."

She stood behind him as he typed the words into a

keyboard. His hair was damp, and she caught a faint smell of perfume, probably from shampoo. As she looked down at him, the line of his neck enticed her, but she resisted the temptation to kiss it.

A message flashed onto the monitors; "Thank you for your enquiry. Please insert Video 418 in Player One, and press Return when ready."

He stood, and crossed to a bank of shelves beside the door. He had to reach up to the top shelf to select the video, and she enjoyed watching his arse tighten to control the stretch of his body.

As he returned, he pulled over another chair, then fed the cassette into the player. He obviously wasn't feeling very talkative, and she sat silently down beside him. They listened to the machines hum as the computer lined up the footage.

After a few moments the lights in the room seemed to dim automatically, and an image of a rocket launch appeared on the monitors.

"The launch of the twin Pluto Probes in 2001 was a significant step in international co-operation to explore the solar system," the video told them. "Twenty Two nations and more than 50 private organisations contributed to the project budget."

Matt hit the pause button. "Our group is one of those," he told her proudly, and he showed her a list on the back of the video cassette.

She leaned over to look and, as she did, put her hand on his thigh to support herself. There was a small creak from his chair as it adjusted to the change in weight.

"That's how we get the direct feed on the probe data," he explained.

She nodded, and let her hand remain lightly on his thigh, as he hit the play button and the video continued.

"The major space exploring nations had dropped the idea of a probe to explore Pluto following failure to fund a mission in the 1980's, which would have reached Pluto as it passed at its closest point to the earth."

The visual was of the concentric orbital rings of the solar system. However Eva was more conscious of the muscles in Matt's leg, which she felt were warming to her touch. Emboldened by this, she caressed the inside of his thigh.

"However the enigma of the planet finally led a coalition of Non Governmental Organisations including NASA to lobby successfully for a project to be mounted through the United Nations.

"As a result of missing the 1980's opportunity however, twin probes were then required for the 'Pluto Express' mission, because by the time they get there, they will fly past so quickly that each will only be able to photograph one side of the planet."

The image paused, and it was overlaid with the message: "If you would like more information on the motivation for the mission press any key, or if you would like to exit, press return."

She looked at him.

"I can't concentrate with you rubbing my leg," he told her. His words however contradicted the physical message she was receiving from his body.

"Who needs to concentrate?" she asked, deciding on an assertive approach, and she leaned towards him and brushed his cheek with hers.

She sensed a moment's hesitation from him, and then felt him relax against her, so that the flesh of his cheek was pressed against hers. She enjoyed the flow of warmth between them, and the slightly prickly sensation of the stubble on his face. He rolled his mouth towards hers, and looked into her eyes. The intimacy was seductive, and they were about to kiss, when he suddenly pulled back, and lifted her hand from his leg.

She sat waiting for an explanation.

"Look Eva," he said, "we can't have a physical relationship while you're not initiated. I like you, but we can't kiss, or make love, so let's not get too horny, okay?"

"Why can't we?" she asked.

"It's health reasons'" he said,

"What health reasons?"

"We have open relationships here in the group," he explained, "and there's a quarantine period before anyone can join us."

"Open relationships?" She savoured the taste of the words, trying to appreciate their meaning. "So you all fuck one another?" she asked.

He grinned. "Not all at once."

Her eyes rested back on the monitor. The instruction was still on the screen, and she pressed a key to give her mind something to do.

The visual jerked back into life. "The small changes in orbital characteristics of each planet have been calculated in relation to the gravitational pull of the other known planets. And these show that either Pluto is far heavier than we suppose, or there are other planets in the gravitational system."

Again the presentation paused, and another continue, or exit, message came up on screen.

This didn't interest Eva, and, because she felt frustrated with his "don't touch me" approach, she determined to push him a little further.

She typed Return, and the system reset.

He looked at her. "Let's have a look at a press file on the group," she suggested.

Without a blink, he keyed in the command, and a menu of dates came up on the monitors. The earliest was 1998, almost 7 years ago.

"Let's take that first one," she suggested.

A newspaper article appeared with the headline; "*Cult goes underground in the wake of Government legislation.*"

She scanned the text beneath it.

"A Kings Cross commune known as 'the Dream-group' which, until recently, has been constantly seeking publicity for their activities, has suddenly shut its doors, and is reportedly going through an 'internal process of re-organisation'."

"Following the mass suicide in Texas, and the gas attacks in Japan, the government here in Australia has been pursuing legislation to register and monitor cults and cult practices. And as a result, many cults are now apparently changing their practices to avoid definition under the act"

"The Kings Cross Group is reportedly going to subdivide the warehouse apartment complex which it owns, dividing the ownership among the group members to avoid the 'collective' clause in the legislation. They also propose to draw up a charter of rights for members, to demonstrate their support for what they called 'democratic freedoms'."

"The Minister disputed whether this would affect registration. "It's not enough to pretend," he told a meeting of Cabinet today. "It's the actual practice that the officers will evaluate"."

She looked at him. "Have you seen this stuff?" she asked.

He shook his head. His eyes were a little wider than usual, she thought, and this encouraged her to talk about her feelings. She felt resentful that he had invited her, and yet had rejected her advances. "Why have you been coming on to me, if we can't have a relationship?" she asked him directly.

"We can," he told her. "But only if you become initiated."

"If I become initiated...." she repeated, as the meaning slowly sunk in. "I'm not going to do that."

"Well, why have you been coming on to me then?" he asked in his turn.

"You can't have a personal relationship outside the group?" she asked.

He shook his head. "I wouldn't want to," he asserted, but his tone belied his words.

"Let's look at something else," she suggested, to change the topic.

He returned the system to the menu, and they chose a date in the late nineties; *"Cult agrees to registration of technology and software,"* read the headline.

"Agents acting on a directive from the Censorship Board for Electronic Media today raided the premises of the Kings Cross cult know as the 'Dream-group', and impounded unlicensed virtual reality equipment and some unique designer software."

"The group had initially denied the existence of the equipment, or of their alleged experiments with virtual reality programming of group members."

"However within hours of the impounding, the group had negotiated a deal with the authorities to monitor and licence their activities."

"What the Kings Cross group has done is develop the software to respond to unconscious impulses from the brain of a sleeping person," the professor of media sciences from the University of Technology explained to a seminar last week. "This enables the virtual experience to occur during sleep, as if it were a very real dream."

"However the dangerous part of this is that there have been no studies on the long term effects of this sort of 'therapeutic experience', which is how it is being described."

Eva glanced at Matt, but he was absorbed in the article.

"The specifics of the deal with the group is yet to be revealed publicly, however it is rumoured to involve registration of equipment; review of software; some form of registration of consent from participating group members; and development of a public manual for the operation of the system."

At the bottom of the screen was a reference. "REF: Virtual Manual # 3402." Eva was warming to the investigation. "Let's check that reference," she suggested.

"I don't think we should," he said.

"Why not?"

"I don't know. I just feel maybe we shouldn't be doing

this."

"Why not?" She was genuinely surprised that he had reached the limit so early, but pleased to have provoked a response in this way. "You gained access with your card, so it must be okay, and now the system is suggesting a reference?"

He turned away and mumbled something which she couldn't catch.

"What was that?" she asked.

"Don't push me," he shot at her. Their relationship had changed gear several times in the past few minutes, and she decided not to challenge him any further.

Having said this however, Matt looked self-conscious. And then, to cover his feelings, turned back to the keyboard and sullenly punched in the reference number.

"This file can be accessed in either virtual, video, or book form," the message read.

"Let's look at the book," she said.

He stood and, crossing to the bookcase, ran his finger along the backs of the books in one of the shelves, until he found the one he wanted. He pulled it out, and dropped it in her lap. It was quite a heavy volume.

"*Registered manual for Virtual Technology and Software at location 42, Kings Cross, Sydney.*" Eva opened the cover. The next page was headed with the word "*WARNING*" in bold letters.

"*The Government of Australia has laid down regulations*

for the use of virtual technology and software. This announcement is inserted under these regulations to inform users of the virtual system at location 42, Kings Cross, that by law the operators of this system must secure your written agreement to participation in on-going use of the system. [Occasional participation by way of introduction to the system is excepted from this requirement]."

"Further this agreement must be freely given, after the consideration of any question, that the participant may have. This manual must also be available at all times to participants, and any new additions to the system must be reported and licensed."

Matt was pacing up and down the small room. "How about I leave you to look through that one, and I'll come back in ten minutes?" he asked.

"Would that be allowed?" Eva suddenly felt nervous about being caught in here by herself, without his authority.

He shrugged. "Probably not."

"Have you looked through this before?" she asked, holding up the manual.

He shook his head.

"Don't you want to?"

He shrugged. "I'm not the sort of person to look in the manual. I just try it. If I like it, okay."

She leafed through the pages. It would take a good

deal longer than ten minutes to come to grips with the information it contained, and anyway she had enough to think about.

"I'll come with you now," she told him.

The meeting hadn't gone as either of them had expected, and she felt the taste of disappointment in her mouth as he showed her to the door.

"Ask Pearl about the initiation," he reminded her, but there was a tone in his voice which warned her that although he did have real feelings for her, there was something more to the suggestion.

Pearl's Decision

Eva awoke to the sun shining through the leaves of the plants in the window-box outside her window. It was patterning the room with leafy shadows, and she lay half dreaming for ages, soothed by the dance of morning sunlight.

An image of her first meeting with Matt, came back to her. Pearl had introduced them she remembered, and there was something very seductive about the way he had looked at her, even that first time.

Maybe he looked at all the girls like that, she thought. She rolled over, her fingers touching the fur of her teddy bear, and she pulled it close and buried her nose in it.

Moana was eating breakfast in front of the television,

when Eva got up. The long sleep had done her good, and she felt much clearer than she had for days.

"I see Pearl didn't come home last night," Moana said. "Did she stay at the group again?" She turned down the sound with the remote control.

Eva nodded. "She'll meet us for the sound check at Darling Harbour."

She put on the kettle, and sat down at the table. Her pack of tarot cards still sat there from the day before yesterday.

We'll have to get going soon," Moana said.

Eva looked at the clock. It was almost eleven, and the sound check was not till 12.30. "We've got some time," she said. She picked up the cards, unwrapped them, and started to shuffle.

"I just want to be there in good time," Moana said.

Eva raised her eyebrows. Moana normally had a bit more of a relaxed attitude to these things, but she looked a little hung over this morning. "Did you go out clubbing last night?" she enquired.

Moana nodded, but seemed disinclined to talk about it. "Good dancing," was her only comment, and she grinned and looked coyly down at her bowl of corn flakes.

"I thought you were gutsy to deal to the leader like that, the other night," Eva said, her mind jumping from one thing to another.

Moana looked squarely at her. "Go very carefully in that place," she advised, and the weight of her concern sent a shiver up Eva's spine.

To dispel the sensation, she flipped over a card from the top of the tarot pack. It was the two of cups. A man and a woman gazed at one another over two overflowing cups.

"Did you notice the guy who was dancing with me at the end of last night?" she asked.

"Man!" Moana smiled. "His tongue was hanging out." She scraped the last of her breakfast out of the bowl.

"I went to the library with him yesterday."

"Did he make good use of that tongue?" A dribble of milk escaped down her chin, as she said this, and she grinned and wiped it away with her hand.

Eva shook her head. "They do group sex, so he's not allowed." She put the card back on the deck, wrapped them, and put the pack in the pocket of her jacket which was hanging on the back of the chair.

Moana savoured the information. "Wonder why he was coming on to you like that then?"

"I think he wants to," Eva said. "He's just not allowed."

On the television, behind Moana, tanks were rumbling through some half demolished city, in a scene that reminded Eva eerily of her first virtual dream.

"They're doing some controversial stuff there," she

told Moana, "with the virtual therapy. Seems like the cops have been suspicious of them since it started."

The scene on the television suddenly changed, and she recognised a shot of yesterday's press conference. "Turn it up," she said, and Moana put down her spoon, and flicked the remote.

"And back home on a lighter note," the announcer said. "The Dance Sisters will launch their latest single today with a free concert at Darling Harbour. However at a press conference yesterday to promote their entry into the Australasian Song Awards they found themselves fending off questions about the break-up of two of the trio's lesbian relationship, and about involvement in a Kings Cross sex cult."

Eva sucked in her breath. The camera focused on Moana. "That line of questioning is why we've been forced to speak out in the past about our sexuality," she said. There was a brief cut to an icy shot of Pearl, and the announcers voice cut in. "This last was in response to allegations that one of the trio was involved in virtual sex therapy sessions. However the newest member summed up the feelings of all of them on the issue."

"We sing, we do it very well," Eva found herself saying once more. "I think it's generally agreed that my voice has strengthened the sound of the Dance Sisters, and that we now present a more dynamic, full voiced act on stage. And that's what's important." There was a wide shot of the others nodding. "We all have relationships. I'd like to think that we are professional enough to rise above that, and to produce an exciting performance no matter what."

Eva found Moana looking at her with new eyes, and she realised that she had taken on a new authority in the trio; she had made a commitment for all of them, and now they would have to live up to it.

The living room had french-doors opening onto a small patio-garden, and the late morning sun was still lingering invitingly outside.

Eva wandered out. To one side was a banana palm, which provided refreshing shade during the hot summer months, and on three sides thickets of bamboo screened them from the neighbours.

Over the bamboo at the bottom of the garden, sat the cityscape and Centrepoint tower. It was sufficiently far away from their Paddington terrace for the garden to feel quiet and secluded, but close enough that they could be in town in ten minutes.

The garden was Eva's little haven from the bustle of the world and she sat on the old wooden bench, and allowed the sensations of the morning.

Pearl was late for the sound check, which was unusual, and it unsettled Eva. They were also working on an outdoor stage for the first time, and she found that the sound was very different.

Moana had taken charge however, and Pearl arrived when they were almost finished. She just slipped onto stage, and although Moana withdrew to allow her the usual space, and they completed the check as they normally would, Eva could feel Moana's resentment building.

"Are you sure you got the rest done okay?" Pearl asked when they finished.

"No thanks to you," Moana told her.

"Shouldn't we run through it one more time?" Pearl asked.

Moana rolled her eyes, and, before they could discuss it further, she leapt off the stage and walked across the grass towards the sound desk.

"Are you okay?" Eva asked Pearl, wondering what she had been up to in the night.

"Sure," she replied, staring after Moana.

The sun was bathing the grass in front of the stage, and a few families were already spreading out their blankets and their picnic lunches in anticipation of the show. There was also a sizeable proportion of lesbian couples, reflecting the strong following which Pearl and Moana had built up.

Moana was leaning over the sound desk, talking with the technician, and beyond her Eva's eye caught the sun shining off the metal framework of the Exhibition Halls.

"Did you do another dream last night?" she asked.

"Look, I don't want to talk about it," Pearl said tersely. "I don't have to."

Eva retreated quickly. "Okay," she said, her hands up in an open palmed gesture. "Just being friendly."

Pearl grunted, and they stood in silence, allowing time to resolve the imbalance that they both felt. The moments seem to stretch into one another.

Moana was still chatting with the technician. "Is she organising to check it again, or what?" Pearl asked.

"It was fine Pearl, really," Eva reassured her. But Pearl just made a face, and leapt down from the stage to stride off across the grass, and find out what was happening. Eva followed her.

"Let's go to a cafe at Harbourside," Moana suggested, as they approached. "It's over an hour till we're on."

Pearl's nostrils flared. "You know I don't feel okay unless I check the whole rig," she said.

"You should arrive on time for sound check then," Moana told her.

"We can't go through it again now," the technician told them, "I've got two more acts to check before 1.30."

Pearl's face coloured visibly and, without another word, she turned and stalked off towards the Harbourside shops and cafes.

Eva looked at Moana.

"Let her blow off steam," Moana advised.

They eventually found Pearl at an outdoor cafe, with a jazz trio busking in the background. As they joined her, the saxophone and drums fell silent and the bass player did a solo, getting some great sounds out of his big acoustic instrument. Eva applauded as she sat down.

"They're not so good," Pearl grunted. "Look at their crowd, it's so ragged."

"God, you're a grump today!" Eva told her. She could feel Pearl's attitude twisting about in her stomach.

"See if you can do better?" Moana suggested. She was naturally more dismissive of Pearl's emotional dramas.

"Bet I could." Pearl rose to the challenge, as she always did, however at that point the saxophone swung back in with the bass, raising the volume. "If there wasn't so much noise," she added, leaned back in satisfaction.

The arrogance of her body language was too much for Eva. "What is it, Pearl?" she demanded. "What's happening with you?"

Pearl looked at her, without however seeming to see her, and for a moment Eva wondered if she too was uncertain why she was behaving as she was. Then something seemed to focus in her mind, and her attention returned to the lunch time bustle about them.

"I'm going to be initiated into the group tomorrow," she told them.

Moana's face froze, and there was a moment where they each considered the implications of this decision.

Eva felt rejected, after all her efforts to bridge the gap between them, and she also found herself feeling apprehensive for her friend's welfare.

"What does that mean?" Moana finally asked the obvious question.

Pearl shrugged. "I commit to being part of the group. It's like a marriage."

"And you live there?" Eva asked.

Pearl nodded.

"Which means we'll have to find a new flatmate?" Despite her earlier cockiness, Moana seemed shocked.

Pearl nodded again, and Moana waved a waiter over, and ordered a neat whiskey.

Eva found her herself fondling the pack of tarot cards in her jacket pocket. She took them out and unwrapped them.

"I thought you weren't drinking before we performed?" Pearl challenged Moana.

"Look who's talking about professional responsibility," Moana shot back. She shook her head. She had developed a drinking problem last year, and had brought it under control, but was still very touchy about the topic.

"I was in the library yesterday with Matt," Eva said, as she shuffled the cards. She was both chatting to smooth out their feelings, and also trying to discuss her real concerns. "Have you checked out the files there?" she asked Pearl.

"No."

"I was reading the stuff about the problems they've had with the cops and the virtual equipment."

Pearl smiled. "Those old stories."

Seeing Pearl's flat rejection of the topic, Eva changed her tack. "Will the initiation change how we work together?" she asked directly. This was her main concern.

Pearl held her gaze for a moment. "I don't see why it should," she said. And the reply hung in the air between them, without, however, the feel of much substance.

As if to dispel this, Pearl impulsively stood and, drawing Eva to her feet, initiated a dance routine from their show. It was a high energy number, and Eva's heart was beating strongly as they sat down again some moments later.

She noticed the waiter looking queerly at their behaviour, however she felt their old camaraderie in Pearl's impulsive action, and this heartened her.

The storm seemed to have now passed for Pearl, and she looked lighter and more alert. However Eva wasn't convinced that her initiation wouldn't effect their work together, because her involvement in the group already had.

"What does the initiation actually involve?" she asked.

Pearl held her gaze with a look she couldn't quite read. It seemed at once eager, and hesitant. "I was going to ask you to come tomorrow," she finally suggested, "I need a partner to give me away at the ceremony."

Despite her misgivings, Eva felt a rush of warmth for her friend. "I'd love to," she said, her sense of rejection assuaged by Pearl's invitation.

Moana was shaking her head in the background, however Eva was saved from acknowledging this by the arrival of her whiskey.

The effect of the alcohol, together with the emotional release which Pearl was experiencing, soon created a light headed feeling around the table.

Eva dealt out a spread of cards. The Fool was in the issue position, stepping happily off a cliff into the unknown. And in the outcome position, The Tower, thunderbolts blasting asunder the crown of the dark castle.

Change was in the air, she realised, and so it wasn't surprising that her world felt like it was beginning to fall apart.

The jazz trio finished, amidst applause, and Moana jerked her head in their direction. "Now's your chance," she teased Pearl. And in her voice Eva sensed again the real depth of the relationship between the two of them, even now.

Pearl smiled at the challenge and, as if to dispel her former angst, she leapt to her feet and bounded over the rail which separated their cafe from the main promenade.

Eva gasped. She had to admire the way Pearl threw herself so fearlessly into things.

"There's nothing we can do to change her mind," Moana advised quietly, once Pearl was out of earshot.

Eva nodded. She knew this to be true.

"She's got to make her own mistakes," Moana added, and there was a broken edge to her voice, which told of the strain, even now, of allowing Pearl this freedom. "I just don't think you should get too involved."

Eva reached out and rubbed her shoulder. "I'm just trying to support Pearl too," she explained, to which Moana nodded.

Already a group of women had stopped to watch Pearl, and, recognising them, Moana waved. They smiled and waved back.

Eva's attention returned to the tarot cards. She let the images filter into her consciousness, providing a lens for her experience.

Then she became aware of chanting.

"Moana, Moana, Moana, Moana..." Moana's friends had begun to chant her name. Eva saw her chest swell with pride, and yet at the same time her shoulders seemed to shrink from the challenge. She had no choice however, and eventually she got to her feet, and lumbered over the railing to join Pearl.

Eva watched her friends launch into one of their old numbers, and smiled. There was a good audience now, and she enjoyed the sensation of watching the show from the outside.

She had done so much street work herself, when she first left home, that she felt no compulsion or desire to join them, and her eyes returned again to the tarot spread on the table.

Suddenly, however, she found Pearl pulling her to her feet, and in a moment they were over the railing with Moana.

Looking to the others for a cue, she found them improvising on the rhythm of their next single, and she started counterpointing some of the notes. This was a great way to warm-up, she thought.

Pearl had a rhythm which she could just turn on, and soon she was pounding out the beat with her feet, and Eva felt her concerns dissolve before the manifest success of their partnership.

They finished and there was applause.

Eva looked at her watch. They had fifteen minutes to get over to the outdoor stage. She glanced back to find the waiter waving the bill for the drinks, her tarot cards still spread on the table, and she had to smile at the weirdness of it all.

7 Initiation

Eva paused at the entrance to the dream-group, and found that she really had to screw up her courage to step inside. The drunk who was asleep in the adjoining doorway, and the stains of wine and vomit on the pavement however, helped encourage her to step into the clean, ordered reality which was to become Pearl's new home.

As she reached the top of the stairs she found Matt waiting there alone.

"Where's Pearl?" she asked.

"Getting ready," he told her. He kissed her on the cheek, and she was surprised by the moist texture of his lips on her skin, and again by the faint smell of perfume or deodorant from his body.

He led her along the hall, passed the open door to the dream-studio with it's busy cubicles, to a closed door marked initiation room, and motioned her to enter.

She peered cautiously inside, and found a room dominated by a stained-glass window of a spacescape at the far end, and what looked like a receptionist's desk, but was more probably some sort of altar, standing in front of it.

"You're lucky to be allowed in here," he told her as the door closed behind them. "This part of the centre is only for inner-initiates."

His smug acceptance of a right to special privileges gave her an almost overwhelming urge to tickle him, but she contented herself with poking out her tongue.

She felt nervous, and her eyes rove restlessly about the room. It was bare and unadorned, except for a row of chairs along one wall and a large painting hanging in the middle of the other, an impressionist landscape with the texture of brush-strokes clearly visible.

"Once you become Pearl's partner, you'll have more access," he said.

"What do you mean, Pearl's partner?" she asked.

He looked surprised that she hadn't mentioned it. "By taking part in the initiation today you become her partner," he explained.

"What does that mean?"

"You just witness that she's entering the group of her own free will." He tossed off the answer with a casual movement of his head. "Then you come to some feedback sessions with her, to check how she's going."

That seemed okay, she thought.

"And in return you get pre-initiate level access, and increased dream control." It sounded like a cross between a sales pitch, and an excuse. "And until then," he finished, "I'm here as your chaperone."

It all sounded like a children's game, and this time she did tickle him, and suddenly his aura of authority popped, his model's chest crumpled in defence, and he tried to hold her arms and stop her.

She giggled, and wriggled out of his grasp.

The expression on his face told her that this was not the sort of behaviour which was allowed in the initiation room, and, to acknowledge this, she sat down in one of the chairs.

He followed her lead. She felt confused about the nature of their relationship, sensing tender feelings from him, but also manipulative games which prevented her from trusting him fully.

As they waited, the painting caught her eye again and, although she couldn't quite decide what it was, something disturbed her about it. The feeling grew, the longer she looked at it.

The pattern of the clouds had changed, she decided after a few moments, and her mind scrambled for explanations. Perhaps it was a dream, she thought suddenly, and she turned to Matt.

"It's computer generated," he explained, sensing her thoughts. The words sat there, heightening the virtual feel. "It's a multimedia screen, programmed to evolve the picture to avoid boredom."

She laughed with relief at understanding what had disturbed her, and the sound seemed to break through the trance of the room.

Just then the door opened and the leader entered. Her presence immediately filled the room, and, as her eyes found Eva's, she felt herself pinned by the contact, her sense of identity melting before the power in the other's look.

Pearl entered next, her head bowed, and an ecstatic look on her face. Eva tried unsuccessfully to catch her eye, as she paced after the leader. It was as if she were either in a trance, or too embarrassed to meet Eva's look. Either way, Eva felt worried, and disappointed by their lack of contact. She had come to support her friend, but was suddenly alienated by the ritual nature of the proceedings.

The moments stretched out, as the two of them paced towards the table, but finally the leader took up a position behind it, and Pearl stopped in front, her feet planted firmly on the floor, her body strangely still.

"Jasmine Jones," the leader began, and Eva felt a slight shock at hearing Pearl's real name.

Pearl also shuffled nervously.

"Place your hand on the bible," the leader told her, and Pearl reached out to put her hand flat on the table in front of her.

The table top must contain a commuter interface, Eva decided, because the landscape suddenly disappeared from the multimedia screen, and was replaced with an enlarged print of the palm of Pearl's hand. Her name appeared above it, followed by her nick name.

Eva watched the image of the hand refine itself into an identity pattern of finger prints, and her blood type appeared beside it.

"State your exact date, time, and place of birth," the leader told her, and Pearl intoned the information.

The data appeared on the screen as she spoke. Then a circle was drawn underneath, and the machine proceeded to divide this into twelve parts. Symbols appeared, and lines were drawn connecting them in various patterns. The machine was calculating her astrological chart, Eva decided.

This was followed by a buzzing sound, and a card popped out of the interface on the table. Pearl lifted her hand and picked it up, but the file image remained on the screen behind her.

Eva was mesmerised by the combination of the ritual nature of the proceedings, and the efficiency of the technology. Then she felt Matt tugging her to her feet, followed by his arm around her waist, as he guided her gently over towards the others.

On the table was a document, around which she suddenly sensed the whole event hinged. Pearl was signing it, and Eva realised for the first time that she had a role to play in the proceedings, and was about to be called upon to enact it.

Pearl put the pen down and smiled at her, acknowledging her presence for the first time, then leaned forward and kissed her.

In the touch Eva sensed again the sisterhood feeling for her friend which had brought her here, but at the same time this expression of affection was so out of context that she found it even more unsettling.

As she stepped up to the table, her heart was pounding. The leader was staring at her with a look she didn't like, glaring through her, and leaving her as if naked before her.

Eva tried to return the gaze, but the more she did, the more she felt drawn into the leader's power and, to break this cycle, she looked down at the document on the table.

She felt too intimidated to even read it, she realised, at which her natural rebelliousness made her pick it up, and she played with it nervously.

There were two copies, she discovered, which had been pressed together so that it seemed like one. The cover was printed in a fine type which was almost impossible to read. Even the heading was hardly larger than normal newspaper print, and she had to hold it up to read it;

'Registration of Consent'.

This must be what the cops had forced them to get participants to sign, she realised. She opened the first page.

'We the undersigned, hereby agree to the clauses outlined herein," she read. This was followed by Pearl's signature, and a pencil cross where she should sign.

Matt leaned over her shoulder and pointed to the pencil mark. "Just sign there," he told her.

She looked at him, seeking the reassurance he was offering, and yet found herself unbalanced by the apparent hollowness of his role. She wanted to trust him, but felt that she couldn't, and so she jabbed him lightly in the ribs with her elbow, to release the sense of embarrassment between them.

The spark returned to his eyes with the physical contact. "If you dare," he challenged her. And the pressure of the moment felt so great that the room seemed to twist, as if reflected in a bent fun-park mirror, the faces becoming elongated with the strain.

The easiest thing to do would be to sign, and get it over with. But still she hesitated. And, as often happens at moments of crisis, time seemed to slow down.

She glanced up at the leader again, to find her eyes

still staring through her with an expression like the wind, pushing her to get on with the "formality" of signing. She desperately wanted to believe that it was all okay, but the whole nature of the proceedings seemed to speak of delusions, and manipulation.

"I'd like some more information on this, before I sign it," she said, bracing herself against the wind, and feeling the eyes begin to burn, rather than blow. And yet, as she said this, she suddenly felt powerful, because she knew she had legal rights.

The moment dragged on, and Eva sensed a desperate need from the leader to maintain control of the proceedings, the chaos of the universe yawning behind even the slightest challenge to this authority.

Finally the leader motioned Matt around the other side of the table, and they bent their heads together in something like a football strategy session.

Released from the confrontation, Eva turned with the document, intending to talk to Pearl, but discovered her absorbed in the file on the screen.

For a moment she realised that there were no eyes on her and, impulsively grabbing the opportunity, she prised the two copies of the agreement apart, and dropping one, slipped the other down the open collar of her shirt as she bent to pick up the first.

Turning back to the table, she found that no one had seen her. She put the first copy back on the table, and the movement seemed to draw the leader's attention back to her.

For the first time she felt the strength to hold the leader's eye contact, however her look was so mesmerising, that when Eva opened her mouth she couldn't remember what she had wanted to say.

Then the leader started gesturing to her, and each time as Eva tried to read the gesture she appeared to break it off, to begin something completely different. She was alternately intimidating, and friendly, changing from one to the other at a moments gesture.

Then she blew gently at Eva, and after a moment she felt herself falling backwards, seemingly without the ability to move her arms and legs. The sensation lasted an eternity, and then she landed in someone's arms.

Matt had caught her just before she reached the floor, and she found her heart was pounding, as he helped her back to her feet.

Pearl was standing by the table looking at her. "What's the go?" she asked, with a look which seemed to accuse her of betrayal, and Eva felt pinned by the stare, wanting to protest her innocence, but unable to make sufficient sense out of what was happening to know what to say.

The blood rushed to her head, and she felt her cheeks burn. As if in a dream, she saw an image of a cliff-top and, crawling close to the edge, she felt herself look over and saw the waves crashing onto the rocks far below. Something started to fall. It was her keys, and she desperately tried to reach them, almost slipping and falling in the process, but in vain, and she watched them disappear.

Then her focus returned to the expression on Pearl's face, and she realised that something would be lost forever between them if she didn't sign the document now.

This insight made the decision simple, and she turned to the table, and picked up the pen.

Starting to Crack

A teenage girl appeared before Eva in the confusion of the record store. Her face shone with pleasure at their meeting, and the open adoration made Eva's heart race. The girl was offering her a compact disc, and Eva pulled out the cover, and signed it for her: 'Love from the Dance Sisters, Eva'.

For a moment she caught Moana's eye, amongst the clash of colours and energies in the store. "Great being famous, huh?" Moana asked. Her tone was slightly ironic, but she had such a good spirit in her relations with the punters, that the value of the in-store promotion was obvious.

"It's the rich I want," Eva told her, and there were smiles from the people about them. Initially she had felt too sensitive for the meat-market atmosphere of the store, but, full of the first flush of popularity, she now found herself getting off on the excitement of the punters.

In her mind's eye she saw the Dance Sisters arriving in London, and being mobbed by the media as they got off the plane. They had personal security, of course, to keep back the crowds, but the English paparazzi were the worst, and would do anything to get an unusual photograph.

Fans were cheering wildly in the air-terminal as they scurried through to the taxi, and, when they got to the hotel, she couldn't believe the luxury of their room. They had a panoramic view over the Thames, and she counted three bridges before the river curved out of sight.

The vision of London stretched out below them excited her, but she also felt apprehensive about the pressure such success would bring, and she was brought back to reality by the jostling of people about her. They were each offering a disc for her to sign. Their faces, looking annoyed by her day dreaming, seemed to press in on her. She quickly scrawled her name on each cover.

"Where's Pearl?" Angel asked, pushing through the press of people about them.

Eva shrugged. "I haven't seen her," she said. Her mind didn't want to focus on the events of yesterday.

"Y'know she's not living with us any more?" Moana asked.

Angel nodded.

"She's okay," Eva told her. "I'm sure she'll be here soon." Her affirmation had a somewhat hollow ring, and she had to acknowledge that she felt betrayed by her friend, and that she was avoiding the issues this raised.

"Moana said that you signed a contract?" Angel prompted her.

Eva felt something catch in her throat. After the trauma of it, she hadn't even looked at the agreement, but had hidden it in a drawer with her underclothes. "I've got a copy," she managed to say, fighting against the feeling that she was betraying Pearl, but justifying it to herself by remembering the manipulation she felt at the initiation. "I'll bring it to the gig tonight."

Angel must have seen the strain in her face, for her expression lightened. "Sure," she said. "No problems." She put an arm around Eva's shoulders, and Eva appreciated the support in her grip.

After a while signing the discs became like a repetitive meditation. There was something spiritual in the "tending of the flock" feel to the experience, she thought, as she scrawled her signature on yet another one.

It was warm that evening as she walked to the Basement, and, although the sky was darkening, wisps of cloud could still be seen behind the flash of neon from the street signs.

Matt stepped suddenly out of the shadows as she approached the gig. He was still wearing only a singlet, as if he couldn't hide his chest, even at night.

"I'm coming to see the show," he told her.

She nodded, but found that she didn't really want to speak with him, and so made no further response.

"Can we meet afterwards?" he asked.

"What! Here in the real world?" she couldn't help but ask, and the viciousness of it made him recoil. She regretted it, as soon as she saw his response, but she had to acknowledge the emotions which had inspired her remark. She felt betrayed by him.

He nodded hesitantly. After all the mumbo-jumbo of the group, out here he seemed such an innocent child.

"Let's see how we feel later?" she suggested, which was the best she could offer. "Why don't you come in, and buy me a drink?" she suggested as an afterthought.

He stood looking awkward, which left her uncertain as to his intentions.

"Don't you want to?" she asked.

"It's just that I've got no money," he told her. "Pearl said she'd get me in, but she's not here yet." At the group he looked so in charge, and here he couldn't even play the flirting game. "I just wanted to talk with you before you started," he finished lamely.

She laughed at his humiliation. "I can get you in,"

she told him, "but if I get myself a drink, it won't have the same effect."

He had to smile at her teasing, and she felt her heart warming slightly to him again.

"How come you've got no cash?" she asked, as they walked over to the entrance.

He shrugged. "Normally I don't need any." He seemed to be groping for an acceptable explanation. "We have communal finances at the group, and I get no pocket money for this sort of outing."

"What say you want to go to a film, or the theatre?"

"I never need to," he said. "There's always something happening at home."

Eva had a constricting feeling in her throat, and she shook her head to clear it. They had reached the venue, and she led the way past the bouncers and down the stairs to the ticket desk. The air at the bottom was heavy with smoke; a mixture of tobacco, grass and hashish. Sydney had become the Amsterdam of the South, since they had decriminalised grass.

The woman at the till was the same grumpy old thing who had been there for sound-check a few hours ago, and she dismissively motioned Eva through.

Eva gestured to Matt. "He's with me," she said, and he was duly also nodded through the doors.

The venue was pumping to disco music and already crowded. Lights played over the throbbing mass of bodies on the dance floor, stabbing and spinning, bouncing off mirror surfaces in the walls and ceiling, and catching the groups at tables and crowd around the bar in flashes of still life.

She felt Matt's fingers searching for hers, and at the same time she felt the contract in the inside pocket of her coat, and the combination felt dangerous. She couldn't trust him.

"I'll catch you later," she told him. "I've got stuff to do."

He nodded reluctantly.

"Maybe you can borrow some money from Pearl, and buy me a drink," she suggested. "It is normal, you know?"

He looked so stupid under her attack, that she couldn't resist jabbing him in the stomach in a playful way, but hard enough so that his face suddenly developed a lot of expression, somewhere between pain and wonder.

She laughed at his discomfort, or at her release from taking him so seriously, and then stroked his cheek, before turning and threading her way through the tables. She wasn't normally so assertive in her relationships, and she felt a little uncomfortable following the interaction.

The backstage area was small and grotty, as if all the mess from years of musicians waiting to perform had just been left to collect in the corners, as it probably had.

One wall was covered with graffiti, messages layered over one another by idle hands as they waited for their moment of glory. Beside it a window looked out on a blind alley, the glass in the grey wall opposite reflecting the pale moonlight.

Angel was standing looking down into the alley. She was alone in the room. They were about the same height and build, and although Angel was a few years older, she already had that air of quiet wisdom, which Eva felt could take her a lifetime to acquire. Perhaps it was more of a shield, she thought, than a true representation of Angel's being. She didn't yet know her well enough to know.

"How is it?" Angel asked.

Eva nodded. She had been resting since the sound-check, but Matt had disturbed the calm she had achieved.

"Was Pearl here for sound-check?" Angel asked.

Eva nodded again.

"What was the story about the in-store?"

Eva shrugged. Pearl had just ignored her when she enquired. "I couldn't get it out of her." She pulled out the folded and now somewhat crumpled contract, and placed it in Angel's hand, and, as she did, she had a fateful feeling; here was a key to a puzzle to which she didn't really want to find the answer.

"This is what you and Pearl signed?" Angel asked.

Eva nodded. She was sweating from the sense of deception which she was feeling, and she half expected Matt or Pearl to enter the room behind her.

"You mustn't tell anyone about this," Eva said. "If it gets back to Pearl that I betrayed her..." She left the sentence hanging.

Angel slid the contract down inside the front of her leather pants. You wouldn't imagine there was anywhere for it to go, Eva thought, Angel had such a sexy figure, but the piece of paper melted into her underclothes.

"Don't worry," she told Eva. "After I read it, I'll have a chat with Pearl, and gently remind her of the commitments she has with us."

Eva nodded. That easy she knew it wasn't going to be, but it seemed impossible to explain this to Angel, and she thought she'd just let events take their course.

She was watching Matt dance to the disco music on the crowded dance floor, and it was turning her on. She was sitting on a bar stool beside the door to the backstage area, and she wanted to join him, but the show was due to start any minute.

Then she spotted Pearl, weaving through the crowd,

and felt relieved she had finally arrived. She was lost in her own world, and didn't notice Eva until she was standing right in front of her.

"Hi," she exclaimed.

Eva reached out and squeezed her arm. "Are you okay?" she asked.

Pearl nodded. "I'm great." A smile played around her lips, and her eyes seemed to glow with life. "How long till we're on?"

Eva shrugged. "Now," she said. The scheduled time was fifteen minutes ago, and the steam had been rising from Angel and Moana, but the punters hadn't noticed anything yet.

Pearl nodded, and pushed through the door beside her. Eva let her eyes fall back onto Matt. The beat was teasing the dancers into ecstasy.

"Well, I won't do them!" Eva put her head around the backstage door, and discovered Pearl and Angel almost spiting at one another.

"You're under contract," Angel told Pearl. "And I expect you to pull your weight in this operation, just like the rest of us."

Moana was standing to one side, simply watching.

"I see what's happening now," Pearl said. "I'm thankful that I can finally see it." The words had an ominous ring. "You guys are just limiting my potential with these chores. I've got more important things to do with my time."

Eva pulled her attention away, with difficulty, from the backstage drama. But she felt like she couldn't take much more of it, and she let her gaze sink back into the semi-conscious buzz of the crowd.

It wasn't her problem, she reasoned. She'd done all she could to support each of them. They just had to resolve it themselves.

There was a lull in the beat as the next record clicked in, and Angel's voice could be heard menacingly; "... do that, and I'll bring the law down on you so fast, you won't have a penny to..."

The ultimatum was drowned by the music, but several heads turned towards the commotion with puzzled expressions, and Eva felt their eyes tug at her, as they sought an explanation, and then move on.

Moana stepped out of the backstage area and stood beside her.

"Too hot in there?" Eva asked.

Moana nodded. "They're twisting her up in that group," she said.

Eva shrugged. There was no easy answer, so she made none.

"What do you see in it?" Moana pushed her.

"I don't know," she said. "I'm just going there to be with Pearl. I think she needs our support." There was more to it, but she couldn't explain what it was. She felt small beads of sweat break out on her forehead. "I also somehow feel more alive when I'm there," she confessed. "It feels a bit like when we're performing."

Moana studied her. "You've been there a lot lately," she said.

"Too much." Eva nodded, wiping her forehead with her sleeve.

"Stay strong," Moana told her, seeing her angst. "Maybe, don't go back for a few days."

Eva nodded, more to acknowledge her concern, than to make any promise, and her eyes again found Matt, dancing in the crowd.

Moana noticed him too. "Have they sent a minder for Pearl tonight?" Her voice suddenly had a strong twang.

Eva shook her head. "I don't think so. He told me he was here to chat me up." She smiled. "But he's been doing a very poor job of it so far."

Moana smiled. "Typical man," she dismissed him, "who need's them?" Eva shook her head. Moana was so staunch, there was no point in arguing with her.

Angel put her head round the door. "It's okay, you can come in now." She was trying to make light of the situation, but a tension in her voice bellied her efforts.

Neither Eva nor Moana made any move to respond however.

"Will you two get your asses onto stage!" she demanded. "We've got work to do." Her patience was obviously wearing thin, and they jumped, half playfully, to do her bidding.

The vibe backstage was icy, and it sent Eva into a dither. As a result she tied, and re-tied, her shirt five times, looking in the mirror each time and panicking that it wasn't right each time.

As she stepped onto stage she had a flashback to her first virtual dream, and the chaos of the civil war. Her eyes saw the heaving mass of people in the venue, and she had a sense of how thin, what we call reality, really is. She felt that sinking feeling again, the dread in the pit of her stomach, at the long road we have to take in our growth.

Somewhere in the mass, her nervous mind found Matt's face staring up at her, and the sight of him brought her back to the expectant hush of the packed venue. She took her microphone out of the stand, and looked to Pearl for the lead.

Pearl was shining with presence, and in full command. With a quick glance to each of them, she motioned to the sound technician to start the backing tape, and as the first notes rang out from the speakers, her feet stepped lightly into the routine.

Eva let her feet follow. She felt light in her body today, and enjoyed allowing the sound of the notes to vibrate out through her chest, and using the dynamic of the choreography to kick some energy into the venue. Soon her heart was pumping, her muscles were warm and loose, and her skin felt soft with perspiration.

Sense of Betrayal

The sun was beating down on the flocks of tourists scattered across the cobbles of Circular Quay, and the air was full of the sound of horns from the ferries, and the melodies of buskers. Eva loved the mixture of tourists ambling in the warm sea air, and commuters moving purposely between the ferries and the train station. Here she could loose herself in the wash of other people's lives, and relax.

A waiter appeared suddenly beside her table, and she ordered a mineral water.

The Quay also had a special place in her heart because she had cut her teeth as a street performer here, after she had run away from her mothers depression. She started by hanging around the other performers, passing a hat for them, and taking a percentage of their money for this work. Then sometimes she'd sing some songs in one of their shows, and earn a bit more, and slowly she had learned the ropes.

Weaving in and out amongst the mosaic of passers-by today, she discovered her fathers' voice echoing a constant theme from her childhood;

"At these rates we won't be able to live on the interest any longer, we'll be using up the winnings," He said in his gruff German accent.

In her memory she saw her mother put down her knife and fork. She had chubby hands and short round fingers, and her face had adopted a long-suffering expression.

"Most people be happy to win the lotto!" she told him, echoing Eva's own thoughts, in her broken English. "Most people buy the things they want and enjoy themselves. But all you do, is complain." Again it was a familiar refrain. She had given up on the man, and seemed intent on feeding him to death.

He simply grunted. His plate was so piled with mashed potato and cabbage, that some dropped onto the table as he struggled to cut his sausage. "It's been a curse," he grumbled, and reached to pour more beer into his glass. "Nothing but a curse."

Eva recalled her mother looking helplessly at her, and felt herself drawn into the alliance against her fathers small-mindedness.

There was a clink of change as the couple at the next

table paid for their coffees, and then the waiter placed her mineral water on the table. She took a sip, enjoying the bubbles, and the slightly salty taste.

Her mother had resented her Father when he was alive, but after his heart attack she had been crushed without him to interpret the strange Australian world to her.

Eva had tried to support her emotionally for a while, but then both their lack of money, because the lottery winnings were legally tied up, and her mother's overwhelming fear, had finally felt like they were stifling her, and running away had, perversely, seemed the safest thing to do.

A girl in tight shorts paraded past, followed by three guys staring fixedly at the movement of her hips. Their faces were a picture of inner fantasy. The sun was hot, and Eva moved her chair slightly into the shade of the umbrella, sinking back into the hum of the flow about her.

"Can I join you?" Matt appeared beside her table, breaking suddenly into her anonymity.

Her blood raced with surprise and, without thinking, she ran her hand up the back of his leg and squeezed. The gesture caught him, in turn, by surprise, and he quickly sat down to hide his embarrassment. She smiled, enjoying startling him, as he had startled her.

He was looking well presented today, having swapped his usual T-shirt for a more formal button-up cotton variety, and brushed his mop of hair back with gel. "I don't let just anyone grab me like that," he told her.

"The way you've been coming on, I didn't think I was just anyone."

"You're not," he agreed, looking at his feet,

"You just happened to be strolling along the Quay, and saw me ..." she prompted him.

He smiled, considered agreeing for a moment, then shook his head. "Pearl suggested you might hang out here in your time off."

"How is she?"

"She's feeling much better." He looked directly at her. "She had a Feedback session this morning, and now she's resting." His eye contact gave the exchange a directness which spoke of honesty, but somehow the words felt a little too practised.

"Is she really okay?" she challenged him.

"Come tonight, and ask her yourself." He leaned slightly forward as he made this suggestion, and this assertive attitude hinted to her that there was more to the meeting than just their emotional relationship.

"Are you under instructions to be here?" she asked.

Still caught in the eye contact, his face coloured as he searched for a response. "I'm to keep an eye on you, because you're important to Pearl," he admitted. "Which is fortunate because I really like you," he added, with a rush of emotion which spoke much more of honesty than his eye contact.

She had to smile, in spite of her misgivings. "And yet you betrayed my trust," she accused him. She couldn't help but confront him with it.

He developed a quizzical look on his face.

"This partner stuff with Pearl... You avoided telling me what I was getting into, and then you let the leader hypnotise me into signing it."

Her emotions were becoming aroused at the memory, and with them went any attempt at melting into the wash of energies across the cobbles about them. There was a crash of crockery in the background.

"It's just a formality," he waved it off, leaning back in his chair. "It doesn't mean anything."

She shook her head. "You'll have to do better than that," she told him.

"It's just theatre," he said. "Look Eva, there are things you can't know, until you're a member." It felt like he was letting her deep into his emotions to validate what he was saying. She still had a sense, however, that there was something else that he wanted to say, but couldn't. And after awhile it began to feel awkward.

"Look Eva," he said again, "everything I do with you, I do with your best interests at heart."

She studied his face, and knew somehow that there was truth in this statement. Something in her softened at this discovery. He may be misguided, she thought, but she could trust his intentions after all. That was important.

She reached across the table and their fingers intertwined, and delighted in each others touch.

"Can I get you anything?" A waiter was suddenly standing beside the table, and the abruptness of it startled her again. How long had he been listening? she wondered.

She shook her head. She still had the mineral water she had bought earlier to validate her seat at the cafe, and it stood untouched before her.

She released Matt's hand, picked up the drink, and took a sip, and he studied the menu. Then he motioned to something, and the waiter bobbed off between the tables.

She appreciated the effort he had made to find her, despite the circumstances. "I'm sorry we missed one another at the end of the show last night," she told him. "I just had to get home."

He nodded. "Pearl and I left soon after you."

She found herself wondering about their relationship, trying to visualise them in the open relationships that he had talked about in the group.

"Have you two made love?" she asked a little coyly,

and she felt vulnerable because she was certain that the jealousy she was feeling must be obvious.

He shook his head. "There's a quarantine period of six weeks before new members can start sexual relations."

"Oh!" She wondered suddenly how Pearl would handle heterosexual relationships. "Do you allow lesbian and gay relationships?"

"All varieties." He nodded. "We just have to be really careful of STD's," he explained "otherwise it spreads through everyone."

The waiter snuck up on them again, and placed a bowl of fruit salad in front of him.

He pulled out some coins and paid for the food.

For a moment she succeeded in loosing her thoughts in the wash of people about them. She caught images from the flow; a ridiculously large sun hat on a red faced man; a cute ass in bike shorts; but through these images something bobbed in and out of her attention.

"What is this session that Pearl was doing this morning?" she asked.

She sensed immediately that he didn't want to talk about it, for he picked up the fork and poised it ready to attack a piece of fruit.

"You mean the feedback?"

She nodded.

"Are you into astrology?"

"Not really." She shook her head. "I think I'd like to be."

"You should come to the evening tonight then."

"Why?"

"It's on Life Cycles," he told her. "It's a good one for getting the basics of astrology."

"That's the second time you've suggested the lecture," she reminded him.

He smiled. "Anyway, you know that the position of the planets at the moment of birth, gives a map of the potential of a person's life?" he asked.

She considered it. She couldn't really get her head around what he meant, however she decided to suspend her judgement to allow him to continue, so she nodded.

"As the planets move, day to day, they trigger cyclical growth patterns which are inherent in each of us," he said. He was on firm ground here, and his confidence had returned. "So in the group we monitor these cycles to assist members to understand the experiences they're having, and to best benefit from them."

It seemed plausible enough. She watched him plunge his fork into a strawberry. There was a precise aggression in the movement which held her transfixed for a moment.

"The feedback is like a counselling session based around issues in your chart," he summed it up, as he put the fruit in his mouth.

"You find it useful?" she asked.

He nodded, savouring the taste.

"Is that what attracted you to the group?" she asked.

He considered his answer for a moment, then shook his head. "It was probably more the sex," he had to admit.

She smiled at his openness, and this encouraged her to probe a bit further. "So are you there for life?"

"I've lived there almost two years now," he told her. "I just decide each year whether to stay for another one." Again she had the sense that there was something else he wanted to say, but couldn't.

She waited to see what might come.

"I see what I'm learning from the leader, so I stay," he said, as if to fill in the gap.

She sensed that he was avoiding something however, and this emboldened her still further. "Is there a status thing, so the longer you stay the more status you get?" she asked.

He shrugged. "In my case, that's true."

"And if you wanted to leave, how would you do that?" she pushed him.

He shrugged again. "There's nothing I want to leave for. There's nothing I can't do right now, if I wanted to."

He seemed to believe it himself, but she sensed from the changes in Pearl's behaviour, that forces other than personal will were at work.

"Well, let's go back to my place then," she challenged him, and she watched him squirm as if pinned like an insect by her attention.

Eventually he took another mouthful, without answering.

"Don't you want to?" she persisted.

"You know I can't," he told her.

"Exactly," she crowed.

He stared for a moment at the wash of pedestrians. "We all have to live within the rules of the community we're part of," he said.

She nodded. "Maybe."

Someone bumped into his chair, and he moved it out of the flow. "Look, can't we just enjoy ourselves while we are together?" he asked.

It was her turn to loose her thoughts in the flow of people past them; two blond backpackers talked loudly to one another, feeling safely private in their foreign language; and a bag-lady poked in the rubbish tin by the sea railing, fishing empty cans out with a bent coat-hanger.

She felt overwhelmed with her feelings, and trying to come to terms with the confrontation that the group's way of life posed for her. "I think I'll go for a walk," she told him.

He nodded. "So are you going to come tonight?" he asked.

"I guess I will," she found herself answering, and then wondered why she had said it. She shrugged off the sensation. "I'll see how I feel," she told him.

He nodded. He'd made his play as well as he could, and he relaxed back in his chair.

She ruffled his hair as she left. She liked him. She let the vibes of the pedestrians brush against her as she walked, and felt the buffeting of different egos, and different worlds, all washing around together. The flow pushed through between newspaper stalls and the ferry wharves and then congregated around a street theatre show.

She caught a glimpse of a group of performers waiting beside the pitch for their turn to work the best spot on the Quay, and for a moment she wanted again to be part of the crew, playing in the streets to earn their living, but her life was different now and she let herself go with the wash.

In the end it threw her up against a railing looking down on the slap of the waves against the harbour wall, and she stood looking out across the water for what was probably several hours.

10

Space

Eva found Pearl in an alcove off the entrance hall. There was a big crowd at the dream-group tonight, and the flow of people eddied about them.

Pearl smiled. She looked fresh and purged of her angst of the past few days. "I'm better now," she said. "I'm sorry I flew off the handle with Angel. I've been quite strung out recently."

Eva reach out and rubbed her arm, to show that no apologies were needed, and they hugged one another. The warmth of her body gave Eva a welcome sense of comfort and safety, and she savoured their contact.

"It should be a good lecture tonight," Pearl said when they eventually released one another.

Eva nodded absently. She had been trying to find a way to voice her concerns about the group, but hadn't really been able to sort out her feelings.

113

"I met Matt down at the Quay today," she began.

To which Pearl just nodded.

"He said you did something called Feedback this morning?" Eva watched her drift away in her mind at the mention of the session, and somehow her feelings seemed to boil over at this lack of response. "Pearl, I'm really worried!" she confided in her friend in a whisper.

"There's nothing to worry about," Pearl said.

"But you're changing, in ways I think you don't realise."

"How?"

"You're more volatile, blowing up at the slightest thing."

"I'm always like that." She grinned.

"You're not as committed to our work. You're missing sound-checks and in-stores."

Pearl shrugged. "I'm there when it matters." She stood firmly on the balls of her feet. Eva had seldom seen her so grounded.

"Look how you're standing," she said, grasping at straws for evidence her friend couldn't refute.

"What about it?"

"You're normally bouncing around. I've never seen you this docile."

Pearl grinned. "So, it's a problem when I'm stressed out, and also a problem when I'm relaxed. You can't have it both ways." She ruffled Eva's hair, and the patronising nature of the gesture aggravated her feelings further.

Just then, however, there was an announcement that the lecture was about to begin, and they joined the movement towards the hall. Tonight it was set out with rows of seats like a theatre, most of which were already full as they entered. However Pearl led the way without hesitation through the mill of people, until eventually they spied two empty seats together.

As they squeezed their way down the row, past the endless pairs of legs, Eva noticed what looked like finger indentations on the ends of each chair arm. She checked as she sat down, just a casual touch with her finger, and a shudder went down her back as she recognised them as virtual terminals. She folded her arms across her chest.

"What's the VR stuff for?" she whispered.

"There's going to be some entertainment later," Pearl said, without looking at her.

Eva flashed back to her introductory dream session, and she felt a little paranoid about releasing herself again to the control of the virtual system. She didn't have to touch them, she reasoned.

The video screen had been moved forward and up on an angle, so that it hung suspended over the front seats. The feed from the probes were still updating data on the mission in the top left hand corner. It was now just over a week to the Fly-past, the display informed them.

"It's popular tonight," Eva said, seeking comfort in the size of the gathering. The obvious interest seemed to validate the experience.

Pearl smiled and nodded. "This was the first lecture I came to," she said, and Eva recalled her being invited to an information evening, a month or so back. It had seemed so innocuous at the time, that she had hardly marked it in her memory.

Then the lights dimmed, and the babble of conversation in the hall slowly died.

The video energised, and the visual opened onto a vista of stars, the sudden vastness of which, gave Eva the sensation as if all the doors had been opened at once, and a gust of air caught in her throat. The visual zoomed in towards a planet with a reddish tinge, which grew larger and larger until it raced past and off the edge of the screen, seemingly so close that several people in the audience ducked.

Another planet could be seen approaching, but the perspective of the screen then pulled back and up, so that, within moments, the cyclic movement of all the planets was visible. In the middle the sun burnt strongly. Four tiny words appeared in one corner and, in epic Hollywood fashion, grew larger until they covered the whole screen;

'Living with Life Cycles'.

There was a surge of music, a sort of symphonic

crescendo, and the image on the video paused. Eva looked to see who was running the system tonight, but she couldn't see the control table. A spotlight came up on a lectern to one side of the screen, and the leader stepped up to the microphone.

"I'm very pleased to welcome so many of you here to our session on Life Cycles," she began, and she seemed to pause longer than was necessary before continuing.

"How many times in our daily lives do we hear the phrases; 'Mid-life crisis', 'identity crisis', 'seven year itch', and the like?" she asked. "Phrases which speak to us of the innate understanding that we all have about the cycles which operate in our lives." Her voice sounded oily smooth.

Eva found the formal nature of the presentation comforting, like being at the movies, and she allowed herself to relax.

"We say; 'I'm at a turning point,' or 'This is a new beginning,' the leader continued. "And what astrology teaches us, is that the movement of the planets in the sky, when related to their positions at the moment of our birth, map out growth cycles in each of our lives."

The video gathered momentum again, and the perspective glided down to follow a planet with rings. "These relationships are called transits, and as we learn to differentiate and understand these cycles, we can use the opportunities they present for maximum advantage."

The leader motioned to the planet on the screen. "Saturn transits represent the areas of our lives that are being challenged at any particular time by the structure and responsibilities of the lifestyle we have created for ourselves."

Pearl moved restlessly in her seat beside Eva.

"Saturn takes 28 years to circle the sun once, and breaking that into its four angles, we get the seven year cycle, with which we're probably all familiar." She paused as if waiting for agreement, and then continued. "This is the cycle which creates the seven year itch, when the structure of our lives may be challenged in some way, and we may want to break away from habits, or activities, or relationships which seem to inhibit our growth."

She motioned from the visual, to the audience, in an expansive gesture. "Is anyone here experiencing a Saturn transit that they would like to share with us?" she asked.

The lights in the room came up slightly, and her eyes swept the gathering. There was no response for a moment, and then suddenly Pearl stood up.

Eva shrank back in her seat, and experienced a sense of heightened awareness of the passing moments.

The leader however seemed to have expected Pearl's involvement. "For regulars in tonight," she introduced her, "this is Pearl, a new member of our family."

Pearl's horoscope replaced the visual on the screen, and a microphone was passed down the row, from hand to hand, until eventually Eva found herself passing it reluctantly to her friend.

"As you can see from the chart, Pearl has Saturn transiting square Uranus," the leader continued. "Saturn represents our responsibilities, and Uranus represents our need for change." She turned back to Pearl. "How have you found the two of these together?"

Pearl shook her head from side to side, and let a sound escape from her flapping lips. The microphone amplified this, and the sight was so comical that there was widespread laughter.

Eva found herself also giggling.

"As some of you know, I work with a singing trio, the Dance Sisters," Pearl began, then paused.

Her words confirmed Eva's worst fears, and increased her sense of vulnerability.

"We signed a new management deal a few months ago," Pearl told them, "which has given us a lot more promotion and performing work. Although I love the excitement of the performing itself, I used to do a lot more of the management, and without this my involvement with the trio is a lot less exciting, and a bit oppressive, like normal work."

Every head in the room was turned in their direction, and Eva felt like a helpless participant. She sighed. She wished Pearl would just sit down and leave the dramatics to everyone else, but that wasn't her style.

"I started the Dance Sisters because I enjoyed the excitement of live performance. I guess it gave me an outlet for my crazy energy." Pearl's face grappled with what to say next. "But much of it's actually a grind, and with the growing success comes more demands. And just dealing with the demands of that promotional work, it takes your whole soul, and turns it into a commodity."

As Pearl revealed more of the intimate details of the trio, Eva felt more and more compromised by the experience. Now everyone in the hall knew of their personal problems.

"So the Uranus energies have come bursting out a few times in recent months," Pearl said, "with somewhat unsettling consequences." She glanced at Eva.

Eva felt something in the look which told her more than all the words. By placing value in the dream group, and publicly airing the dirty linen of the Dance Sisters, Eva felt that Pearl was sending her a message, perhaps one that even she hadn't consciously realised. Pearl was leaving the trio, Eva felt, because her life was taking her in a new direction. And as much as she loved Pearl she was going to have to let her go, and she felt herself choke back the flood of emotion she felt at the realisation.

"Recently however," Pearl continued, "I've found the stuff here has given me an opportunity to change my life in a liberating and exciting way. And I think that has given me a new outlet for that Uranian energy." She sat down, and the microphone found its way back along the row of hands.

The leader's eyes panned over the audience, and someone closer to the front stood, and the process was repeated.

As each person revealed their personal experience, it seemed to bond the mass of people in the hall, closer together. The sharing of personal experience in relation to astrology also started to make it real for Eva. The correspondence between each persons experience, and the astrological indicators seemed incredible. Then the lights dimmed and the video energised again with a visual of a star vista, she looked at the stars with a new wonder.

"If you place you hands on the terminals in your arm rests, your experience of the next few minutes will be enhanced," the leader said, and the light on the podium went down.

Eva felt everyone about her place their hands on the terminals, but she let hers simply rest on the chair arms without actually touching the terminals.

The vista on the screen seemed to pull back, and a spacecraft came into view. She guessed that it was the view of one probe from the other. There was a collective gasp, which she felt must be due to the virtual inputs, because the visual wasn't that impressive. It just looked like any picture of a satellite.

She glanced at the people around her. She could see no real change in Pearl or the others, except perhaps that their faces seemed more animated than a few moments ago, and so cautiously she touched the terminals herself. She was instantly flooded with the sensation of being actually out in space. It wasn't an unpleasant sensation, just something totally different than the confinement of rooms, buildings, and streets.

She jerked her hands away. The room felt flat and oppressive, after the sensation of space, and she found she actually wanted to replace her hands. She made herself comfortable in her seat, and touched the terminals again.

There was the vastness, something like the Australian outback, nothing for as far as the mind could reach. Her attention was caught by the craft however, and to her surprise she found she could decipher the pre-programmed commands that it was executing.

She felt its transmitter shut down, and then the rockets fired briefly. She watched it align itself with what looked like a large dark star, which she guessed must be Pluto. The technical majesty of the mission left her in awe. The transmitter came back on, and a steam of data flowed back to the waiting ground receiving dishes. At the top of the screen the co-ordinates and distance data monitors flashed the new information as it came in.

The experience was a bit like a horror movie, or a roller coaster ride. Eva felt glued to her seat by the shock of experiencing the vastness of the universe without the comforting filters of her daily life. Then she realised she was holding her breath, and had to consciously breathe to regain her balance.

She pulled her hands off the terminals. About her the hushed auditorium pulsed with the experience, and in the darkness, but the sensation of the chair and the other solid objects about her, she found comfort. She brought her knees up and sat cuddling herself while the show played itself out. She felt alternately proud that she had the strength to opt out of the experience, and a hopeless failure because she was not like all the others. One thing was certain, she didn't want to touch those terminals again, and find that emptiness out there.

"It just made me feel so insignificant," she told Moana later. "And then walking home I became so frightened." She had found her waiting up, when she returned.

"I thought you weren't going to go there for a while," Moana said. She was sitting under a doona on the couch, watching the television with the sound down.

Eva felt so relieved to be safely home that she discovered she was shaking. She went to shrug, but she was shaking so much she found it difficult to control her movements, and they both burst into laughter at the absurdity of it.

"You look like you need a cuddle," Moana said, lifting a corner of the duna. Eva felt a rush of warmth for her friend, and she collapsed on the couch beside her, crawled under the doona, and was comforted by Moana's soft body. She lent her head on her shoulder, and could smell the oil in her hair. Slowly the trembling subsided.

"Angel wants to see us first thing in the morning," Moana said.

"We can't get Pearl there now," Eva said, knowing it would be impossible to get a message to her until tomorrow.

"She doesn't want Pearl there," Moana told her.

Eva nodded. It must be the initiation contract, and she felt a surge of guilt.

Moana must have felt it, because she ran her fingers lightly across Eva's forehead and through her hair. Eva closed her eyes and enjoyed her touch. Moana's fingers stroked the tension from her mind, and within moments she fell into a deep sleep.

Monsters in the Dark

Angel paced over to the window of her office and stared down at the harbour. "I've had this thing checked by a couple of experts," she said, waving the initiation agreement. She considered her words for a moment, then shook her head. "It's pretty deadly." Her expression, reflected in the tinted glass, was a mix of disappointment and a sort of calculating cunning. "So we have to tread very carefully." She looked like a cornered animal.

Moana was sitting in almost the same position as the other day, her fuzzy mop of hair silhouetted against the panorama of the harbour. However the clouds were now building in the sky behind her, sweeping in over the sea, to bank up as they encountered the city.

Eva felt responsible for allowing Pearl to sign the thing, and the deliberate caution of Angel's comments annoyed her. "What does that mean?" she asked.

"Well, for one thing," Angel turned to her, "they want your money!"

Eva experienced the information like a punch in the guts. She couldn't believe it, and, to prove her point, Angel walked over and showed her a section of the text.

"The partner agrees to place all tangible assets at the disposal of the group, if so called upon," Eva read, "to underwrite loans to support the initiates progress." Her experience with the dream-group had all seemed weird, and yet nothing had prepared her for this discovery. She felt aghast, and grabbed the document, to read further; "This clause shall also be interpreted to cover any assets realised or acquired after the signing of this contract and during the period the Initiate is a member of the group."

Behind Moana the darkening clouds seemed to form sinister shapes, which glared in at their window with a menacing intent. Moana reached out for the agreement, and Eva handed it to her.

Angel sat perched on the front edge of her desk, and her head darting slightly forward and back in a rhythmic movement as she processed her thoughts.

"Can they do that?" Eva asked. She suddenly felt afraid of loosing everything that was deer to her, and the feeling seemed to be welling up from beneath the carpet underlay, and in danger of flooding the room.

The boss simply nodded.

Moana was studying the text. "Did you read it, before

you signed it?" she asked, and Eva felt so victimised by the whole thing, that she felt small tears well up in her eyes.

"No, I didn't," she replied. Her heart beat increased defensively. "I couldn't."

"Why not?" Moana pushed her.

She simply couldn't find the words to explain, and the tears in her eyes grew with the frustration.

"What's your interest in them?" Angel asked her, and the accusing tone of her voice put Eva further on her guard. She felt in shock, and there was a long pause, while she didn't reply.

"You said you feel more alive when you're there," Moana prompted her.

Eva kicked her leg playfully, but still without making any response. She didn't know what to say, and for some reason she felt like she should defend the dream-group. This feeling seemed so ridiculous however that she had to laugh, and the action seemed to release her inhibitions, even though it sounded a little hysterical. "I'm just trying to help Pearl," she told them. "And you guys aren't being very supportive!" The tears started running down her face. It made her feel like a child.

Angel tossed her a tissue. "Did you ask anything?" she asked. "Or did you just sign it?" She seemed impervious to Eva's emotion.

"Yes, of course I did." Eva felt herself getting angry. "I

said I wanted more information."

"And?" Angel was like a blood hound on the scent.

"The leader just waved her hands around." she groped in her memory. "And then I fell backwards, and Matt caught me. And when I stood up Pearl was looking at me like I was the enemy. For not signing. So I did." She shrugged. "I figured I could trust Pearl."

She watched an indecent smile spread slowly across Moana's face, an expression born of much experience. "That was your mistake," Moana said.

Eva wanted to hit her, to pummel her with her fists until she softened. She couldn't believe that Pearl had betrayed her knowingly. She probably hadn't read it either, she decided.

"You're just so twisted with hate and resentment," she told Moana, "you've got no faith in anything any more." She knew it was an unjust thing to say, but she was disturbed by Moana's mistrust. "Don't you see that she needs our help, not our judgement?"

Moana pursed her lips in a little pout, but made no other response.

"Otherwise she wouldn't have signed this thing," Eva pursued her.

"Come on guys," Angel cut in. "Instead of getting into this personal stuff, let's use the time to understand this thing." She motioned to the agreement in Moana's hand.

"What else makes it deadly?" Eva demanded, wiping

the moisture from her face.

"It's mainly for Pearl," Angel said. "It ties up her personal management, so that she has no personal control over any aspect of her work with us, and then can't benefit financially from it."

"Can they do that?" Eva asked again.

Angel shrugged. "Just as you can agree to hand over your money," she said, "she can agree to hand over management of her affairs."

"But I didn't agree to it," she said forlornly.

Angel shrugged. "Tell us about the ceremony?" she suggested.

Eva told them what she remembered, and as she talked she alternately reached into her memory to recreate the experience, and now and again studied the faces of Moana and Angel for feedback to what she was saying. Angel had a detached professional attitude which she found reassuring, but Moana had developed a look of fascination, and Eva found that she had to avoid her eye contact after a while, otherwise her sense of betrayal of Pearl would have been too strong for her to continue.

"I'm sure a good lawyer could get you both out of it," Angel said for the umpteenth time. They had agonised over the situation for hours, but Eva still found it hard to know exactly what to believe.

"The agreement wasn't entered into freely from your side," Moana tried to explain, "so it can't be enforced." Sunlight was breaking through the clouds outside, broad shafts of yellow light, which seemed to throw a halo around her head.

"It's more Pearl I'm worried about," Angel repeated. "She's really tied herself into it." She walked round the desk to sit in her chair. "Why would she do that?"

"I don't think she wants the responsibility to tie her down any more," Eva suggested, without really knowing how she knew this.

"She's a big gal anyway," Moana said, releasing Pearl to her fate, "she can look after herself." Rainbow glimpses of colour teased across the split-ends of her hair.

Angel shook her head. "It's not that easy from our side." Often she seemed daringly flippant with her big schemes, but in her current deliberate thoughtfulness, Eva sensed the real strength behind her success. "We need her to fulfil her contract with us."

The clouds closed in again, and as Eva's eyes adjusted to the new light level, Moana's face returned from the shadowy land of silhouette. She caught Eva's eye, and Eva sensed her evaluating the strength of their partnership.

"Perhaps we don't need her," Moana suggested.

"Of course we do!" Eva exclaimed. A sense of

foreboding again filled the room. Pearl was central to their work, and she just couldn't imagine the Dance Sisters without her.

Moana shrugged. For her, Pearl was obviously expendable. "So what's the strategy boss?" she asked Angel.

Eva found their manager looking directly at her. "You've agreed to attend some sessions with Pearl?" she asked. "Something called feedback sessions."

Eva nodded. She felt heavy from the emotions of the meeting. "It's something to do with astrology," she explained. "Something like a counselling session." She groped for the words. "There's one tomorrow," she remembered. "But..." A shudder ran down her spine. "I don't want to go now."

There was a pause. "That's why I was asking about your relationship with the group," Angel said. "Because it would be good if you could go... If you feel up to it, because it will help keep us in touch with Pearl, and I think that's going to be important."

Eva shot Moana an "I told you so" expression, and for a long moment they looked deep inside one another, caught in the intimacy of shared life experiences. Eva's anger had washed in like a wave, empowering her to confront her friend, and then it washed away to leave her vulnerable and open to Moana's response.

Moana, however, held her attention without

indicating any response, and with each passing moment they seemed to reach a new level of intimacy. Eva felt the muscles in her face twitching with the release of tension, and then finally they reached an equilibrium, where they both knew that they were on the same team.

Eva found herself giggling with relief.

"We've got a big week in front of us," Angel told them, "and the more we can work together to make it happen, the better."

They both nodded.

"Perhaps you could go with Eva to this session tomorrow, for example," Angel suggested to Moana.

Moana's eyes widened at the thought. "You've got to be joking."

Eva found herself wondering whether it would help to have her there, or just be something else to worry about. "It's okay, really," she said to ease the situation, but with their new found intimacy she knew her insecurities about the group must be apparent, and she watched Moana steeling herself up to a decision.

"Yeah, I'll come with you," she said, with a little too much swagger to be taken seriously, and they all burst into laughter.

Eva loved her in that moment, as she reached out to embrace experiences that she wouldn't choose herself, for the sake of her friends.

12 *Feedback*

Eva's heart was beating strongly, and she took Moana's hand as they entered the feedback session.

"Hey Moana!" Pearl greeted their entry. "Didn't know you were coming." She and Matt were sitting side by side on stools at a small round table, which was the only piece of furniture in the room.

"I wasn't," Moana told her ambiguously.

The sparse furnishings, together with the indirect lighting on the walls, gave the room a sacred feel. Eva let Moana take her seat first. There were three spare stools at the table, and she chose to sit with an empty one between her and each of the others.

This left Eva to choose between sitting beside Matt or Pearl, and she took the closest stool, which happened to be beside Matt. She hadn't yet eaten today, and her stomach rumbled as she sat down. She quite liked the feeling of being hungry, it made her feel light and alert.

"How are you?" Pearl asked her.

Eva welcomed her friend's attention, but found no easy answer to her question, so she simply nodded in response. Pearl continued to look at her however, as if she expected more of an answer, but Eva found it too hard to articulate her feelings any further. She actually felt deeply wounded by her dealings with both of them, but she wasn't prepared to confront this, and her silence seemed to make her an accomplice in the deception.

"There's a lot happening?" Pearl put words into her mouth, and Eva nodded again. She was a bit in shock, she realised. She drummed her finger nails against the smooth grey opaque material of the table top to release her frustration.

Matt placed his hand on hers to stop her. "It's a plasma screen," he cautioned, and then she noticed the key-pad which was set into the table by his seat. The possession of these controls always gave him a superior attitude which she resented, and she poked him in the ribs to release her feelings.

He let out a grunt of surprise, and the look on his face was so comical that both Pearl and Moana laughed.

The leader entered at that moment, and the mirth settled in the room as she walked around the table. She moved with a magnetism which communicated on a physical level, and seemed to challenge a response from

134

each of them.

Eva felt her shoulders tense.

As the leader sat in the empty seat between Pearl and Moana it seemed that the communion around the table instantly evaporated. Pearl was drawn physically closer by her presence, and Moana leaned back on her stool, as if away from the fire.

Matt's attitude also changed. His body sat more erect and his eyes were wider. He seemed to be admiring her every move, and Eva realised that his allegiance to her was very strong.

Then she felt the leader's gaze turn to her, and she found herself transfixed by the raw emotion generated between them. She tried to relax under the force of her attention, and found that once she accepted the natural authority it carried, she felt a strong sense of security in the relationship.

"I am your life and your death," the leader told her, and Eva nodded as if this was self evident.

Then she caught Moana's expression, and something in it made her stop. "She just said, that she was your life and your death," Moana repeated.

Eva nodded. Then thought about the words. "Well, perhaps that's a bit of an exaggeration," she agreed.

The leader bowed her head.

"She means it symbolically," Matt whispered. "As a newcomer she takes responsibility for you, as if she were your life."

Eva nodded, but Moana looked unconvinced.

"Pearl can you insert your card?" Matt requested, and she slid something into a slot in front of her.

He punched the keys to energise the table surface, and her chart appeared, the lines between the planets highlighted in different colours, the patterns stretching out between them and creating geometric shapes on the table top. Eva found herself trying to decipher the symbols, but with no knowledge of the system, it was just a meaningless pattern, however she found them a safe place to rest her attention after the rush of contact with the leader. She stole a glance at Pearl, and found her also absorbed in the chart.

Matt tossed cards labelled "visitor" to both herself and to Moana. Eva picked one up, and slid it into a slot that she found in the side of the table. He typed into the keyboard, and her name appeared on the table-top in front of her.

"Could you put your card in?" he asked Moana. It lay untouched on the table. Her attention was fixed on Pearl and the leader, and she ignored his request.

In her mind Eva had an image of their garden, the fronds of the bamboo rustling in the breeze, and, realising that she just wanted the session resolved as soon as possible, she reached across and slid Moana's card into the next slot.

The leader was looking at Pearl, and Eva noticed her shift in her seat after a few moments, to sit more upright, and to straddle the chair with her legs. The position made her small breasts press through her shirt provocatively.

"Let's do relationships today, shall we?" the leader asked her, "since some of your closest friends are here?"

Pearl nodded imperceptibly.

The leader signalled to Matt with a small motion with her hand, and the image of the chart on the table dimmed, and then one of the symbols shone out brightly. It was the symbol for female energy, a circle with a cross beneath it. Slowly the whole mandala rotated so that this symbol sat in front of Pearl.

"This is your Venus," the leader told her. "Which represents your values and relationships." A symbol beside the one for Venus also glowed. It was a circle with a dot in the centre. "You have Venus together with your Sun," she told Pearl. "This is an aspect which gives a desire for inner peace and harmony. It's a sign of a romantic, somebody who loves beauty, poetry, and art."

Eva could easily see that in Pearl.

Then a red line rolled straight across the table to a point between Eva and Moana, and two more symbols illuminated. One looked like the number four, and the other like the Venus symbol with the circle cut in half and a smaller circle nestling on top.

The leader's eyes lifted from the chart, and held each of them for a moment. "However the Sun/Venus conjunction stands opposite a conjunction of Pluto and Jupiter," she continued.

It felt a little like a seance, Eva thought.

The leader gestured to the two planets beside Eva's elbow. "Jupiter and Pluto together give an intense longing for exciting experiences, and probably transformative experiences. It's the opposition between them which adds the tension to these two different sides of your personality. The longing for exciting experiences works against the peaceful romantic. The two needs pull in opposite directions."

Eva nodded. That was definitely Pearl. Moana seemed to be growing more and more on edge, however, as the leader accurately assessed Pearl's character. Eva could tell this from her steady eyes, and the tension she sensed in her body, although her outward appearance was still one of studied indifference.

"I guess I've been trying to get that balance through our work," Pearl suggested, motioning to Eva and Moana, but looking for approval to the Leader.

"But you haven't been very satisfied, have you?" she responded.

Pearl thought for a moment, then had to shake her head. Her eyes found Moana's, and they stared at one another. "Our relationship was also an attempt to balance those needs for me," Pearl told her. "A loving, wild, transformative relationship." She spoke wistfully.

Eva sensed that the leader didn't like this interpretation. "Unfortunately with these aspects there is also a tendency to compulsive attachment to destructive relationships," she said, and she looked at Moana. "Possibly even violent relationships."

Moana sat braving out her gaze, neither flinching, nor acknowledging her challenge. Eva admired her stand, and wondered where she found the strength to hold her own in that way. She noticed that Pearl was watching intently. Indeed, seeing her observing like that, Eva had a sense that the event was stage-managed to demonstrate something to her.

"What I'd like to do, if possible," the leader said, looking from Moana to Eva, "is to key in each of your birth dates, and correlate the relationships with Pearl's planets." She let them absorb this for a moment. "Do you know what time you were born?"

Eva shook her head.

"Look sister," Moana burst out, "I'm not playing your little charade so you can manipulate me with your psychological games!"

The leader absorbed her comment for a long moment. Much longer than was in fact necessary, and the flow of time built-up, and put a pressure behind the leader's eventual response. "I don't think you'll ever have the commitment needed to benefit from this work," she finally said. "And since no-one invited you, and you don't want to participate, you may as well leave."

Moana stared at her, but made no response.

"In fact," the leader continued, "since we don't want you here, I'll have to request that you leave."

Moana looked around the table and considered her options. Both Pearl and Matt were watching her squirm in the trap which the leader had set. Pearl seemed very detached from the drama, again observing as if it were an experience which was designed for her.

Eva felt annoyed at the turn of events. She resented the leader's hold on the others, and admired Moana's stand in the face of such odds. But above all she wanted to resolve the conflict, and this wasn't helpful. "Come on guys!" she said, trying to relieve the tension. It seemed like the first words she had spoken all session, and yet somehow they seemed to fall into the cross-fire of eye contact as if they had never been spoken. Everything was starting to go wrong, she thought.

Realising that she had no other option but to leave, Moana stood, pushing back her stool. "Are you coming?" she asked Eva.

She felt torn by her need to support both her friends. Pearl's look was begging her to stay however, and she felt determined to salvage something from the situation. "I'll be okay," she reassured Moana. "I'll see you at home."

The leader smiled at her, and despite her misgivings Eva felt her spirits lift with this approval. "Would you show Moana out?" the leader asked Matt, and he stood to do her bidding.

Moana took one last look at Pearl. She wouldn't make this effort again.

A small smile, playing on the leader's lips, betrayed her pleasure at this turn of events.

"You don't know your birth time?" the leader asked Eva, when Matt had returned. There was an edge of disbelief in her voice.

Eva shook her head. She suddenly felt vulnerable, without Moana's support.

"But you know the date and place?" the leader pursued her.

She nodded, but felt reluctant to give out this information.

Pearl was watching, as she had earlier, and this waved a warning flag in Eva's attempts to respond. She caught her friend's look, and tried to assess her sincerity. There was a sense of detachment in their contact however, which left Eva feeling uneasy. She was here to help, and yet it felt like she was somehow being betrayed. But, despite this, it seemed impossible to withhold the information the leader was requesting.

"I was born in Adelaide," she told them.

Matt keyed in the data as she recounted her birth information, and allowed herself to fall back into the trance of the soft lights, and focused attention. So long as she did as she was told she felt okay. When he finished the input, another ring was added to the chart on the table-top, and new planet positions came up around the outside.

"It's a grand trine," the leader exclaimed, and they all beamed at her.

Her heart beat picked up momentum.

The leader motioned to three symbols, equally spaced around the circle. "Venus, the Moon, and Neptune," she said. "Which gives a flow of inspiration, creativity and emotions in your life."

"What does that mean?" Eva asked. She had that feeling of dread, that important truths about her life were about to be revealed.

"We don't really have time to go into the detail now," she told her, "as this is Pearl's session."

"Oh!" The sound of her disappointment escaped Eva's lips before she realised it.

"But I'm sure Matt would read it for you later, if you can come another time."

She looked at him, and he smiled, adopting a bedside manner which looked too studied to be real. But she resisted poking him in the ribs, and held his eye contact long enough to feel the strength of his feeling for her, underneath the acting, which left her confused as to her own feelings for him.

"What's interesting for us to see," the leader told them, "is the relationship between Eva's planets, and Pearl's." A new set of lines criss-crossed the table. "Particularly the conjunction of Eva's moon and Pearl's Saturn." She pointed to two planets which were almost on top of one another.

"This shows what an important role you play in Pearl's efforts to shape her life," the leader told Eva. "You smooth out the edges and lighten up her experiences." This acknowledged something Eva felt instinctively, but which was never articulated, and she appreciated the leader bringing it to their attention.

"And you in turn provide Eva with an opportunity to live out her emotions," the leader told Pearl, in turn. "Which is a responsibility which you must not take lightly."

Pearl looked at the leader while she digested this information, and then, when she turned to Eva, she had a new interest in her eyes, which shocked Eva with its suddenness. Where she had been feeling a yawning gulf developing, there was again a friendly contact, and yet at the same time this seemed to validate her effort of coming. This was the outcome she had wanted.

The leader motioned to Matt, who punched some

keys, and a print-out of the chart data began from a slot in the table beside his seat.

"We can probably let you go now," the leader told her, "while we finish a few things with Pearl." Eva felt as if she had accomplished her mission, and been released, and she hopped lightly to her feet with a sense of relief. The fronds of the bamboo from their garden again waved in her mind. The printout chattered to a stop. "Can I have a copy?" she asked.

There was a dead silence in the room. It had been an innocent question which demanded a natural yes, but seemed doomed to a certain no. Matt shook his head. "This one goes on file, so it's available for the feedback sessions," he said. "I'll print you out another when we go over your chart."

She nodded, but was left unsettled by the response. Any challenge seemed to break through the veneer of conviviality in their interactions, to hint at the underlying tensions.

13

Pearl Splits

Eva stumbled as she stepped into the venue, and the toes of her right foot grazed on the step through the open front of her sandals. The pain was intense, and she cursed under her breath, then sat on a chair just inside the door, hugging her knee to her chest and caressing her injured toes.

For a time the entrance foyer seemed to loose definition about her, and she felt alone and unable to adequately deal with the experiences in her life. She wanted to call out to someone to help her, but there was no-one around.

After a few moments the worst of the pain had subsided however, and she was able to hobble past the empty reception desk and push her way through the swinging doors of the club.

It looked seedy without the people, she thought, as

she surveyed the almost empty room. Only yesterday she would have bathed in the excitement of performing in such a well-known venue, overlooking the beer stains and cigarette burns on the carpet, but as she stood in the door, and the stale smell of alcohol washed over her, she felt sick.

"Glad you could make it!" Moana greeted Pearl above the hubbub of the now busy club. Pearl had missed the sound check again, and Moana was obviously going to take it out in sarcasm.

Pearl tried to wither her with a look, but it only served to aggravate her former lover's resentment. They were sitting on stools at the bar, and Eva watched Moana's expression detach itself from the bubbling faces on either side, and firm with a sudden fury.

"We've worked fucking hard to get here," she said, "And you've got to keep your end up, no matter what wanky self-mutilation you happen to be getting off on at the time."

Pearl's expression froze, and then she glanced about, as if in search of support. This wasn't home ground any more however, and there were no guards here to run to her rescue.

Eva instinctively held out her hand, but although Pearl acknowledged the gesture, she chose instead to simply turn and walk off through the crowd towards the backstage.

Moana's eyes stalked after her. "I had to say it," she said, inviting Eva's support.

"But maybe this wasn't the best time," Eva suggested before reminding herself to stay out of the personal stuff between them. As if that was possible!

The evening seemed jinxed however, because there were problems with the mix from the moment they stepped onto stage. First Moana's voice seemed too dominant and Eva couldn't hear her own, and then Moana's faded into the background, and Pearl's microphone started crackling.

Pearl hated technical problems, and Eva could see her shoulders tensing in anger, as the rest of her body proceeded with the choreography. Then her microphone cut out all together, and she just stopped dead in her tracks. Eva caught a moment of the anguish on her face. It was her worst nightmare, for without sound she was as if naked on stage.

Eva and Moana were both continuing with the song however, so the longer she stood like that, the worse it became. Eva couldn't understand why she didn't just mime along with them. Moana had adjusted her voice to fill out the sound, and Eva also allowed hers to flow more into the body of the song.

Feeling the other two take over in this way must have made Pearl feel worse however, for Eva saw the tension build up in her face, and suddenly she threw the microphone over her shoulder and marched off stage.

Eva felt her gut wrench, and she looked to Moana for a lead out of the situation. She was still continuing with the number as if nothing had happened, except that her face was now wearing a wry smile. She was enjoying Pearl's discomfort, Eva realised, and she shook her head, all the while continuing with the song as if on an automatic program.

Then Moana caught Eva's eye, and raised her hands in a comical gesture of helplessness. This sent the right signal to the audience, because they took it as a cue for laughter, probably suspecting the walk-out was actually part of the choreography, and the two of them finished the number to applause.

"Unfortunately we're going to have to take a short break while we fix some technical problems," Moana announced, "but we'll be right back."

Eva followed her off stage. Her heart was pounding. She dreaded dealing with Pearl in the mood she was in, and as soon as they stepped through the curtain her fears were realised.

"I won't stand for sabotage!" Pearl told Moana.

"It's your own fault," Moana replied. "You should

have been here for sound check!"

A technician ran through the backstage area and onto the stage. He gave Pearl the fingers, for her misuse of the equipment, as he passed.

"It'll be fixed in a moment." Eva tried to make the peace.

"Why don't you just shut up!" Pearl rounded on her. "You haven't a clue what's really happening."

Eva felt the injustice of the attack like a pit opening up before her, and her adrenaline raced to her defence, and the blood rushed to her face. "This is our work," she told Pearl icily. "This isn't your personal therapy session." She had never spoken to Pearl in that way before, and as soon as she had said it, she regretted it.

Pearl took a step backwards, looked from Eva to Moana, then spat on the floor. Eva felt her stomach turn in disgust. This wasn't the Pearl she knew.

"That's it!" Pearl declared. "We obviously can't work together any longer!" And with that, she stormed out, and they were left gazing after her in shock.

Eva cursed herself silently for her impulsive comments. Everything she had worked so hard to avoid had been realised by her own hot blooded remark, and she felt guilt gnawing at her stomach, or was it fear of the expectant crowd, who had begun slow clapping outside. "Shit!" She cursed out loud.

Moana shrugged. She had been staring after Pearl

with an expression which was a curious mixture of amusement and worry.

"What are we going to do now?" Eva demanded.

Again Moana shrugged. "Guess we have to cancel," she said, and the ease with which she said it sent Eva further into shock.

"Cancel?" she asked.

"Yeah... Do you want to do the show with just two of us?"

Eva tried to imagine how that would effect the sound, the staging and the choreography, and her mind boggled at the changes needed. She shook her head.

"We'll give them their money back," Moana told her, gesturing to the noise from the venue, "and give Angel a call."

It sounded simple, but Eva's world felt like it was falling to pieces.

She watched the taxi disappear up the hill, and turned for a moment to look out at the yachts on Rushcutters Bay, and then back at the entrance to Angel's apartment block. Moana was holding the door open, and waiting.

Eva suddenly felt an inexplicable dread at the idea of entering the building. "I think I'll walk down to the water for a moment," she said haltingly. "... cool down," she added in an attempt at explanation.

Moana shrugged. "Don't be too long," She said, disappearing through the door. She was so accepting, Eva loved it in her.

The water was breathlessly still, and a gentle lapping against the shore and the boats was the only sound. She was conscious that the foreshore wasn't the safest place to walk at night, however in the thrash of her current experience it seemed a small worry, and she allowed the gentle wash of sound and sensation to calm her fears.

By the time she knocked on the door of the apartment, her mind felt much clearer, but she still had a gnawing sensation in her stomach. The door opened for a moment on the security chain, then closed and opened again to reveal Angel standing in a white dressing gown. She looked strangely vulnerable without the trappings of her office. Her gown fell open slightly as she motioned Eva inside, and Eva sensed from how she retied the sash that she was naked under the garment.

The apartment was a moderately-sized one, and the night panorama of Sydney lay spread beneath the window. Angel liked being high up, Eva noted. Moana was sitting at a table by the window, and Eva joined her. "Feel better?" she asked.

Eva nodded. "The water is so calm tonight."

Angel put a pot of tea on the table beside some cups and a jar of honey, and sat down. "Strange," she said.

They looked at her.

"Calm water," she repeated, with a dead-pan expression. "Strange." Then her eyes twinkled, and Eva felt a sigh heave from her chest, and she found herself laughing.

"Damn strange," Moana agreed, grinning.

Angel started pouring the tea. "We're going to cancel a couple of gigs," she told Eva. "Give everyone a rest."

Eva took a mug of tea, and warmed her hands around it. She marvelled at the way Angel had put her at ease with a simple joke and a clear decision.

"It happens all the time," Angel reassured her. "The demands of the work prove too much, and we all need rest."

"But... It seemed quite final," Eva was hesitant to disturb the rosy picture she was painting, but the image of Pearl spitting on the floor didn't sit easily with the concept of a rest.

"We get the law on them as well," Moana told her.

"We threaten legal action," Angel corrected her. "Hopefully we won't actually need to go to court."

Eva wasn't certain that would help, either way. "It might just make Pearl more obstinate." She looked at Moana for a lead, since she knew Pearl better than anyone.

"She's a funny fish." Moana chewed on her words. "She's always looking after herself first, whatever's happening around her." There was a hint both of bitterness, and admiration, in her voice. "But something worried me when I saw her in that session yesterday."

She looked at Eva for confirmation, and Eva recalled the image of Pearl sitting on the opposite side of the chart-table. The drama and the technology did appear to weave a web around her, a web in which she seemed to sit quite happily, almost a passenger, but Eva couldn't really find any sense of danger, or manipulation of her friend. She shrugged.

"But you can't tell her what to do," Moana continued. "That's the other thing."

"If she's under their influence," Angel said, "we simply pressure them to support her work with us."

"How?" Eva asked.

"We can blow their whole operation wide open if we go to the court with that initiation document," Angel said.

"Which they obviously won't want," Moana added. "So they'll have to do a deal with us."

"I just wonder if we're loosing sight of Pearl in all this drama?" Eva said. "If she's made a decision, maybe we should respect that."

Moana's look etched her concern. "But did she make

153

it of her own free will?" she asked.

Eva found it hard to separate her own emotional need for Pearl to maintain her role with the Dance Sisters, from any fears she might hold for her friend, and then make a decision.

"You've been most closely involved," Angel pursued her. "What do you think?"

"She's definitely doing it because she wants to," Eva told them. "But how much that decision is influenced by the psychological experiences and rituals there, I don't know."

"And if we pressure them for support?" Angel asked.

"That might help," Eva conceded.

"Give us time to see if she is for real in this," Angel explained, "and stabilise the situation with the Song Awards."

Eva nodded, she was right.

"If I get the lawyer to prepare a letter, could you arrange to give it to someone at the group?" Angel asked her.

Eva nodded again. She wanted to talk to Matt about that chart interpretation, but they should probably meet on neutral ground to deal with this business with Pearl first. She needed to adopt a more assertive approach to their relationship, she decided, because she had nothing to loose, as the rules of the group apparently stopped any further development of their relationship anyway.

14

Proposal

There was a taste of raw sexuality in the air. It pulsed with the beat of the music, wove enticingly between the dancers, and then slid, with the clouds of dry ice vapour, out amongst the tables of the club.

Eva savoured it, as she leaned against the wall and watched Moana negotiating her way back from the bar with their drinks. Her jeans were baggy around her hips, but seemed to caress her crotch as she moved, and she was wearing a halter top which hugged her tits and left her brown stomach available. The room was alive, and she was greeted at almost every step by a friend or a lover, the latter making much of the availability of her stomach.

Eva felt out of her depth amongst such overt sexuality, but the heat of the crowd provided her with somewhere to lose herself, and she needed that.

Moana put the drinks down on the edge of a nearby table. She looked like a different person in this environment. Not the partner to Pearl, nor the work comrade who she had known for these past months, but someone exciting and a little scary.

They held eye contact for a moment. Eva made no attempt to hide her vulnerability, and sensing this, Moana reached out and ran her fingers up the back of Eva's neck, squeezing the muscles at the base of her skull.

Eva let her head fall into Moana's grasp, releasing, too suddenly, the up-tightness which was keeping her head upright. She found Moana's face beside hers, felt the warmth of her breath, the softness of her skin, and then they were touching lips, and Moana's tongue was exploring hers.

She felt exhilarated with overcoming the taboo of kissing another woman, and then their lips parted again, and the familiar twinkle in Moana's eye swam back into vision. The wall still felt solid behind Eva, and the swirl of the club was continuing about them. However she sensed an acceptance from the couples about them.

"It's kind of mandatory," Moana explained her forward behaviour. Eva grinned, and reaching over she took her hand for a moment, the touch expressing her thanks for their friendship.

They watched Matt enter the club, and thread his way through the press of sexual energy. He looked quite comfortable in this environment, but was avoiding physical contact where this was possible.

Neither of them made any move to attract his attention, preferring instead to enjoy his progress as lions might from a hilltop. It had been Moana's idea to meet in a gay bar, and she looked disappointed that he wasn't more uncomfortable in this environment.

Some seats became vacant at a nearby table, and Eva moved quickly to claim them. This attracted Matt's attention, and he made his way over. There was an awkward moment as he realised she was not alone, but she distracted him by tossing an envelope onto the table. He looked at it, but made no move to pick it up.

"Are you going to sit down?" Moana asked him.

"Maybe," he said, sitting down.

Above their table a large extractor fan was sucking the dry ice vapour, together with the cigarette and hash smoke, out through the roof.

"Look I'm sorry about Pearl and the shows," he said. He was shouting to be heard over the hum of the fan and the beat of the music. "I've tried talking with her about it, but she's made up her mind." He shrugged.

Eva pressed her lips tightly together. She was certain that Pearl's stubbornness would be the downfall of their plan to lure her back. Then she felt Moana's foot rubbing against hers under the table, and she felt the pressure to play out the strategy on which they had agreed.

"What is it?" he asked, nodding toward the envelope.

"It's from our manager, to your leader," Moana said, grinning broadly at her lack of personal responsibility.

"But you must have some idea what it is?"

"We're just the messengers," Eva told him, feeling guilty at the deceit, but knowing he would do the same with impunity.

A couple of guys pushed their way through the tables arm in arm, and one of them stumbled against Matt as they passed. Matt brushed him gently off.

"What's the idea of meeting here?" he asked.

She couldn't resist the urge to tease him. "Just 'cause you're so up-tight."

"I am not."

Eva felt the beat of the music pulling at her limbs. "Come and dance then," she suggested. She stood up.

"Okay," he responded. The envelope was still on the table, and he picked it up, and put it in his pocket.

She headed towards the dance floor, turning briefly to check that he was following her. The floor was packed with people, and she worked her way into the middle, and relaxed into the surging mass of movement, letting the rhythm drive her body, and enjoying the release this provided.

Matt wormed his way in beside her, and the pressure of the surrounding dancers forced them to dance pressed against one another. She held his waist, and ran her hands over his backside, pulling his pelvis gently against hers. She felt him pull away.

"See," she teased him. "Even here you can't shake off the watching eyes of home."

At which challenge he relaxed back against her, and they played with the flow of sexual energy between them for the rest of the dance.

Later they found themselves pushed more towards the edge of the dancing mob, and Eva enjoyed moving without so much pressure of bodies around her.

She discovered Moana dancing alongside them. Moana leaned towards her, as if to say something, but, when Eva bent her head down, Moana nibbled her ear instead. Eva giggled, and they danced together for a moment.

Matt looked offended at Moana's intrusion, and, seeing this, Moana swapped to dance with him. Eva watched her initiate a game of teasing him by dancing very intimately, and then swapping to dance closely with Eva.

The dry ice vapour was pouring around them. Eva

joined Moana's game, arousing him with her contact, and then flipping him aside.

"It's too frustrating, really," she told him, as they had found another table. "Trying to have a relationship with you." They had a few moments to themselves while Moana was getting a drink.

He grinned. "Join the group," he told her. "We'd be making love in ten weeks."

She choked at the lack of romantic sentiment. "Drop out," she told him, "we'd be fucking tonight."

He grinned. The idea possibly did have some appeal, she realised suddenly, and they held one another's eye contact.

"There is another way," he told her.

"What?"

"We could partner one another in a love-dream."

"How does that work?"

"We imprint one another's dream-unit, to enable the virtual image of the partner to be created."

Sometimes words seemed to hold little meaning, she thought. "Do we do it together, or separately?" she asked.

"Separately," he told her. "It is technically possible to participate in the same dream, but the leader has forbidden it."

Her interest was aroused, but she also saw a funny side to the suggestion. "It's like a wet dream?" she asked, grinning.

He nodded, maintaining his cool as much as possible.

It sounded a definite second best to the real thing, Eva thought, but she felt her juices starting to flow at the thought.

Moana returned with a colourful cocktail. It had a mound of cream on top, with a straw like a paper umbrella. She offered it to Eva, who took a sip. It was cold and sharp at first, but soft on the way down her throat. She passed it on to Matt, who also tasted it.

Moana held his eye contact as he passed it back.

"I wouldn't worry about Pearl," he told her suddenly. "Often as newcomers enter the group there's a period of change in their lives, and sometimes this can lead to quite erratic behaviour."

Moana nodded. "That's what I was thinking," she said. "It seems to me, like you guys are the problem."

He shook his head. "It's in our interest that Pearl keeps working with you."

"How's that?"

"We're all encouraged to take on high profile positions in society, and earn good money," he said, attempting to explain the psychology of the group. Then he shrugged. "Pearl's got some personal thing she's working through."

Eva marvelled at the way he so easily identified with the interests of the group, and at the same time shrugged off any personal responsibility. "Perhaps she needs some help," she suggested.

The way he sprang on the opportunity however, sent warning signals. "It might help to have you with her more often," he suggested, and she felt her shoulders tensing at the thought. "Help to bring her old life with her, into her new one, and maintain that connection."

Moana hissed at him, and he shrank back in the chair.

Eva smiled at her support. "That's what I've been thinking," she told him, "but it hasn't helped so far."

Moana sucked on the straw, and then sent the cocktail round one more time.

He shrugged, and sucked on the straw. The club churned around them. "These things take time." There was a dab of cream on his upper lip, and he licked it clean.

"I would like you to do my chart for me," Eva told him, almost as a concession.

"Any time." He smiled. "We could do it tonight. I've got a car here."

Maybe that's what she needed to give her some insight into the chaotic events of her life, she thought. She looked at Moana, who wagged a finger at her impulsiveness.

Or was there something else developing between them? Eva wondered, and she realised that she didn't want to complicate their relationship in that way.

15

Astro Threshold

Eva felt something tug in her throat as they walked up the stairs to the Dream-group. Mentally she was kicking herself for her impulsive decision to come.

"It was silly to come now." Her nervous tongue had to let out her feelings.

He took her hand as they reached the top, and she found his touch comforting. "It's a perfect time," he assured her.

They passed the closed door to the dream studio. A couple of guys, who she had seen on visits here before, were standing guard outside, and they smiled greetings to one another as they passed. People were very friendly here, she thought, and was again comforted.

"Everyone's at the evening session," he explained, as he opened a door further along the corridor, "so the chart rooms are free."

Following him through, she discovered a little room, in the middle of which was a small table, like the feedback table, which stood between two bar stools. Behind it the view, out between the buildings on the other side of the street, was down onto the harbour.

Matt crossed immediately to the window, and Eva followed him. The lights of the city were dancing tonight, and the moon had just risen, and was hanging ripe and full in the sky. The majesty of the world hung stretched out in front of them, and they found a long moment of peace in its contemplation.

She ran her hand up his back, and cuddled against him.

"This is my favourite room," he told her, taking a card out of his pocket. "Because of the view." He crossed back to the table and swiped the card through a slot in the side, then tossed it back to her.

It was her visitor card, she realised. She put it in her pocket, and somewhat reluctantly left the window and sat on one of the stools.

The table started glowing from the inside, and the surface resolved into a chart image, with her name in the centre.

"The first thing you have to realise is that the chart represents a matrix of potential," he told her. "How you work with that, is your business."

"What's that mean?" she asked.

"It's not black and white," he tried. "It doesn't say whether you are one way or another. It just suggests tendencies, or potentials, and how you work with them is up to you."

She nodded. He seemed to be hedging his bets. Maybe he wasn't very good at reading charts, she thought.

"It's also a delicate mixture of many factors," he continued, "so while one aspect might suggest one tendency, another may counter this."

"I always feel a little cheated by the horoscopes I read in the papers," she told him. "It seems too easy. How can we all be generalised like that?"

"That's because the newspapers are just reading the influences of the sun sign," he said. "Which is the area of 'will' in our lives. Obviously 'will' has a huge effect in shaping our lives, so the sun sign is often very apparent to people."

"But we're all so different!"

"Because there are at least eight other planets, a moon, and various mathematical points which can be interpreted to develop a more intricate perspective of each individual." As he said this he motioned to the web of lines in the circle on the table. "And, because we are dynamic beings, we tend to shift emphasis in our chart, to focus on certain sides of our personality at various times."

"So, where do we start to understand it?" she asked.

"We look for geometric pictures in the relationships between the planets," he told her. "You've got this grand trine between Venus, the Moon, and Neptune, for example, which is going to influence your life, as much as your Sagittarius sun."

"What does that mean?"

"It's this equal-sided triangle here," he said, motioning to a triangle of green lines on the table. "Each of these lines represent a flow relationship between the planets at either end, and when three of these are joined like this, it's called a grand trine."

It sounded like mumbo-jumbo, like a confidence trick. "But what does it mean for me?" she asked.

"With the Moon, Neptune and Venus at the points, it means you have a very sensitive and sensuous placement of these planets."

Suddenly she wasn't sure if he were making fun of her, and she poked out her tongue.

"No, I mean it," he said. "Venus trine the moon, is a person who knows instinctively how to be charming, and is therefore popular, and possibly artistic at the same time."

She felt her body still as a cat's might while eyeing a bird. This was the information she wanted.

"Venus trine Neptune adds tremendous creative potential to this," he told her, "and the ability to get along with everyone, regardless of who they are."

She had always felt comfortable with people, she thought, relaxing into a trance of suspended disbelief.

"And Neptune trine the Moon assists this creative sensitivity further," he continued, "and gives you the ability to bring beauty into your surroundings, to physically manifest art."

"Sounds too good," she said, in a way which invited him to reject her protestation.

"You've got other aspects which aren't as easy," he told her instead. "Like all of us."

"Like what?"

He pointed to a red line though the centre of the circle, joining onto one corner of the green triangle. "Your Moon is opposite this Uranus conjunction with Mars."

"So?"

"The opposition is a tension relationship, with the planets involved pulling apart," he explained. "Uranus opposite the Moon can give a tendency, for example, to misjudge people, and to attract unusual people into your life, with the assorted difficulties which go with each of them."

This information brought her sharply back into the present moment, the surrealist surroundings, and the bizarre nature of their discussion, and she nodded, smiling at the aptness of the description.

He didn't get it. "It can also lead to anti-authoritarian

responses," he continued, "and when paired with Mars, there's a tendency to release pent up energies through social intercourse."

"How's that?"

"It means you have a tendency to provoke responses in others, which can easily lead to arguments, and undermine your own position."

She noticed he was protecting his chest as he said this, and, realising that she did have a desire to tickle him in response to this comment, she grinned and contented herself with kicking his foot.

"And the conjunction of Mars and Uranus itself in the tenth house is a volatile configuration denoting ebbs and flows of energy, and explosive conditions, particularly in your professional activities."

She looked at him. "Why my professional activities?"

"The tenth house is to do with your role in society," he explained. "And Mars and Pluto together is always a bit explosive. However I imagine it might be quite good for performing. Just a bit volatile, and a bit vulnerable to industry back-biting and social recognition games."

She could relate to that also. It was the cliquey nature of the industry which annoyed her most. She was beginning to feel like this was something with the power to shed some light on her life, and she felt a deep excitement.

"Your professional activities will probably also leave

you feeling alternatively like you can't quite handle the demands of the job, and then craving the excitement in the lulls in between the peaks."

She nodded. Performing was always like that.

"And you also have to constantly adapt to the demands of your job," he added, "with the opposition to the Moon."

It made her feel both, a little trapped to have her life defined so clearly by a set of symbols, and at the same time excited to come in contact with this seemingly cohesive explanation of herself.

"I think that could be enough for now," she told him.

"Just before we finish, let me show you how to read it yourself," he said, "and then you can do it any time."

She nodded.

"You book the room in the office, swipe your card to activate the chart, and then, to explore the interpretation, you touch your finger to the area of the chart you're interested in."

He demonstrated by touching the two planets at the end of the red line from the Moon, and a window of text overlaid part of the chart image.

"Mars conjunct Uranus," it was headed, followed by a description similar to the one he had just given her. He touched the corner of the text window, and it disappeared again.

She experimented by touching the line between the

Mars conjunction with Uranus and one of the other corners of the green triangle.

Two text windows appeared; "Venus sextile Mars" read one, and "Uranus sextile Venus" read the other. Underneath this second heading it read;

"Gives a desire to bring harmony and beauty to many people through some form of social or artistic work." and under the first; "A natural born lover with no troubles with members of the opposite sex."

She became conscious that Matt was also reading over her shoulder, blushed, and closed the windows with her finger.

He could probably read it just from the symbols she realised, and the vulnerability of him seeing into her like that frightened her. She got down from the stool and wandered back to the window.

He came up behind her and put his arms around her. And, after a moment, she cuddled against him. "How does it work?" she asked.

"At the moment of your birth, you are imprinted by your first experience of the world, and that imprint is measured by the position of the planets at that moment."

"That doesn't really explain anything," she said.

"I think it's like a strange attractor," he tried again. "It gives shape to our lives by attracting a certain sort of people and events into it."

His conjectures were disturbing the magic of the

moment, and she held her finger up to his lips, to quieten him, and they stood staring out at the city-scape.

After a time he brushed her cheek with his lips. "Do you want to do a virtual swap tonight?"

She felt exhausted, and the idea of trying to negotiate her way home didn't appeal. "How does it work?"

"We just touch each others terminals before we retire, to signal our consent for virtual sex."

"So we sleep separately?" she asked.

He nodded. "And that way you're here in the morning to see Pearl."

It seemed safe enough, she thought. The only apprehension she now felt was her memory of the helplessness from her first dream. "I think I might feel a little raped by the machine," she told him.

He looked shocked. "You control it yourself, with swaps," he told her. "So you couldn't get raped."

Sometimes she found it hard to know what was real in their interaction, and what was theatre. However the warmth of his body seduced her, and, as he slid a hand up and caressed her breast, she reached up with her lips and kissed him on the cheek.

The swap was warm and enjoyable, and, quite in contrast to her first dream, the machine was now manifesting her every whim, and she soon seemed to develop a playful co-operative relationship with it.

It felt like Matt crept into her cubical soon after she fell asleep, and they spent hours making gentle sensuous love, before falling exhausted into a deep sleep.

16

Pluto Approach

The smells of breakfast were wafting through the air, mixed with the sounds of Mission Control as they monitored the progress of the Pluto probes.

Eva was standing just inside the door to the studio, out of the flow of the foot traffic, and overlooked by the passers by, who were intent on the food on the breakfast tables.

Finally she saw Pearl emerge from one of the cubicles and move towards a nearby table. She was walking slowly, and Eva had no trouble catching up to her.

"What are you doing here so early?" Pearl asked, as they sat down.

"I stayed over."

"Dreaming?"

Eva nodded. She found that she didn't want to reveal her swap with Matt.

174

"Me too." Pearl spoke wistfully, as if reluctant to let go of the dream images. Her hand began tapping a rhythm on the table, to the background clatter of breakfast and the chatter of mission control.

Eva poured a coffee, then offered it to Pearl, who nodded. The background voices from mission control gave a surreal feel to the breakfast. Eva passed it to her, and poured another cup.

Pearl seemed to feel no need to explain or resolve anything, despite the fact that their career together seemed to be in tatters.

"You see what I meant the other day about changing?" Eva asked her bluntly.

Pearl nodded. "You were right," she agreed lightly. She helped herself to a slice of toast, and proceeded to butter it.

Eva took a sip of coffee, held it in her mouth for a moment, and then let the taste spread down her throat. Her attention perked immediately. "Is that all you're going to say?"

Pearl looked at her. "We change," she said. "What can I say?"

Eva held her eye contact as she absorbed the directness of her friend's response. "You can explain what those changes mean for the people who are close to you," she suggested.

"I don't know, Eva," Pearl responded. "And it doesn't

help to have you playing 'poor me' all the time around me."

The injustice of it hit Eva like a blow, after all the effort she had made to support Pearl. "I'm here, aren't I?" she asked coldly.

Pearl nodded, and then for a brief moment the old spark of contact was back between them.

"We're taking a couple of days off," Eva told her. "To give us all a break."

Pearl nodded. "Let me know what's happening," she said, sounding conciliatory, but vague in terms of her future commitment.

Eva nodded. She was holding herself back from pushing too far, to give Angel's strategy time to work, and she gulped down some more coffee.

The chatter from mission control increased in volume, and a visual of the control room was played up onto the video screen. A voice began counting down, and on "zero" the screens in the control room went blank, and everyone waited.

Eva noticed that the feed from the probes had frozen at the top of the screen.

"Communications system shut-down, as planned, while orbital rocket firing occurs," intoned a voice. The waiting in the control room dragged on. Somehow it seemed mirrored in the breakfast room, with most people ignoring their food as they waited.

Eva drank the rest of her coffee. She couldn't face any food, she decided.

The leader entered the room with an entourage of followers, and they took their seats at the top table. Still the screens at mission control stood blank. Then a voice started counting down again from ten. On zero however nothing happened, and there was a flurry of activity as scientists checked their equipment.

"The system has maintained shut-down, probably due to orbital adjustment fine tuning," intoned a voice. "There is a fall-back reboot option in one minute."

Eva had an almost overwhelming desire to demand of Pearl whether she was going to do the competition or not, and as she restrained herself she heard Matt's voice echoing in her mind from the chart session;

"It means you have a tendency to provoke responses in others, which can easily lead to arguments, and undermine your own position." And she laughed lightly at the insight she was gaining.

Pearl looked at her, perplexed as to the cause of her laughter.

The count-down started again, and this time on "zero" the system flickered back into life, and information streamed in from the probes computers. There was a cheer from the scientists.

"Probes on track for fly past at 9pm Sydney time tonight," came the voice, and with that the audio faded, although the visual of mission control stayed on the video screen.

"Is the fly-past tonight?" Eva asked.

"Yes. It's a big event," Pearl told her. "I'm doing some performing."

"Where?"

"Here. We're having a celebration." Pearl said. "You should come."

Eva shrugged. "It feels like I live here already," she said.

"I'm doing something special tonight," Pearl told her. "Challenging myself a little." She caught Eva's eye and the slight feeling of fear in her look aroused Eva's curiosity.

Then a woman, who had been sitting beside the leader, stood up, and a hush descended on the room.

"I've just got one general announcement this morning," she said. "We're coming up to the medical check-up period again, and if I could just remind you that when you register to have your STD check with the hospital, try and use another address, so that we don't all look like we live together."

There was laughter.

"And try and develop an original reason why you should want an STD test." There was more laughter. "We'll do two planetary groups a week, starting next week with Mercury and Venus."

Eva looked questioningly at Pearl.

"They're like support groups," Pearl told her. "I'm in Chiron."

Eva hadn't heard of it. "Is that a planet?"

Pearl nodded. "Planetoid," she explained. "Somewhere between an asteroid and a planet." Eva could only nod. "There's eight of us in the group, all newcomers."

"I hope you all enjoyed yourselves last night." The leaders voice rang out, and there was a general rumble of affirmation.

"We had a new sex-swap pairing last night," she announced, and Eva felt herself shrink back inside her chest. "Our trusted Matt has hit on one of the newcomers."

Matt was sitting at the leader's table, and she motioned him to stand.

"Tell us about it," she told him.

He stood, clearly embarrassed. Eva suddenly wondered if the dreams were monitored, or worse recorded. Her heart was beating. She dreaded to see her intimate fantasies up on the video screen for all to see.

"I always find these situations embarrassing," Matt started, trying to clear his emotions by talking about them. "But the fact is, that Eva and I have a particular relationship which I value very much."

Eva darted a sideways glance at Pearl, and found her

179

enjoying the show. It felt as if there were nowhere to hide, and a shiver ran up her spine.

"Of course I've invited her to join our group, but in the mean time we consummated our bond in virtual space last night." He paused. "And for my part it was very good," he added with a smile.

The leader seemed jealous of his pleasure.

"Are the dreams monitored?" Eva whispered to Pearl.

She shrugged. "I've wondered myself."

"Apparently Matt's partner is one of the famous Dance Sisters," the leader said, conferring with someone beside her. "And she is with us this morning."

Eva's heart sank. For a moment she considered making no move, hoping to be overlooked, but Pearl was already helping her to her feet, so she pushed her chair back and stood up. The room was a sea of faces, all turned towards her in expectation.

"How did you find our young stallion?" the leader asked, cuffing Matt playfully on the shoulder.

Eva groped for something to say. She felt awkward expressing her intimate feelings publicly, especially when she hadn't even had time to recognise them herself. And this sense of discomfort became translated into the sarcasm in her response.

"I would have preferred him in live flesh and blood," she said, "without the etiquette of your particular mating system." There was nervous laughter from the breakfast tables.

"But aside from these minor issues, you found him satisfying?" the leader persisted. She was visibly baiting Eva.

"How could I do otherwise?" Eva asked. She'd come out punching, and now had to maintain momentum. "It was my dream, so obviously I'd dream it to be satisfying."

The leader shook her hand as if she'd touched something hot, and there was an in-breath from around the breakfast tables.

The room seemed to grow colder, and Eva had a dry feeling in her throat. She had a sense of kaleidoscopic motion of the room about her, as her adrenal glands gave her a rush, and it felt like she had never been more present or alert.

"You seem dissatisfied however," the leader pushed her. "Perhaps Matt didn't really satisfy you, and you just don't want to admit it to him."

The injustice of her interpretation pushed Eva's emotions to the surface. That wasn't how it was at all, and she stood speechless for several moments, while words of explanation caught in her throat, and then they came tumbling out.

"It's just not very easy to talk about intimate sexual experiences in front of masses of people." Her chest heaved, and, despite her best efforts, a small sob escaped her lips. "It just seems to be a way of undermining my self esteem."

The leader lightly clapped her hands in applause of Eva's comment, which at first she took to be a sarcastic response, until the release from about the tables encouraged her to also relax a little.

"A very personal, and appropriate comment," the leader reinforced Eva, dropping her provocative attitude, and there were murmurs of approval from the room.

"It is hard to share these intimate details," the leader continued, "but this is the very reason why it is valuable to do so." And, as if the clouds had gone, the feeling in the room lifted.

"Which brings us back, as always, to the twin issues of honesty and commitment," the leader told them. "Which is what is required to make any relationship work," she said. "We each know that."

Eva wondered if she should sit, however the leader directed the next few comments directly to her.

"Here in the group we have open relationships, so we must be self expressive, and committed, to make these relationships work. Which is what living in the modern world requires of everyone, of course. However we have grasped this challenge, because we are prepared to face the personal issues it brings up."

Then she directed her attention to the whole room. "This is the difference between Matt and Eva." she said.

"Matt is committed to developing himself. and therefore, to playing an important role in the community."

Matt beamed as the leader held him up as a role model. "Where as Eva," she continued, and the tone of her voice was painfully disdaining, "is still a little caught in the trap of seeking self gratification through the fame game."

"I am not," Eva protested sharply.

The leader looked suddenly impressed.

"I do it for the music," Eva asserted.

"And winning Awards means nothing to you?"

"That's just part of the business, which makes the music possible."

The leader shrugged. "Perhaps you also have the commitment it takes," she said. "But what are you hiding from, if you can't talk about these intimate things?"

This was a valid question, and Eva considered it.

"Maybe you should think again about joining us," the leader suggested. "Because, if you can find the commitment, I think you would really benefit from the experience."

Eva hadn't considered the prospect, but it did seem to offer an exciting opportunity to encounter herself in new ways, and she felt an incredible high from the interaction.

"A big hand for Eva," the leader said, and she found herself beaming at the applause.

She sat down. "It felt ugly there for a while," she said to Pearl, "but then it ended so supportively."

"It doesn't pay to be bolshy," Pearl advised her.

"I just feel confronted in this situation," Eva told her, "and then I want to bite back." She poured herself another coffee.

Pearl shook her head at the inappropriateness of such a response, and there were grunts and murmurs of support from the others at the table.

Eva closed her eyes and tried to centre herself. In all the changes she was loosing her sense of who she really was. She felt Pearl's hand rubbing her shoulder, and although she welcomed the touch, she felt uncertain how to respond.

17 *Stunned*

Eva allowed her body relax back into the soft cushioning of the chair in Angel's office. Moana was sitting in the one beside her, teasing knots from her hair. Outside the window, the clouds were unsettled and a little electric.

"This old lady was walking across the road in front of me, as I was driving in," Angel told them. She was sitting casually on the front of her desk. "Then she just stopped in the middle, looked straight at me, and lay down on the road."

"So you hit the gas and flattened her," Moana suggested ironically.

Angel shook her head. "It was a one-way street. So I just stopped, and hit the horn."

Eva was still feeling high from the confrontation with the leader, and this allowed her a sense of detachment from the experience about her. So it was left to Moana to play audience to Angel's story.

"What happened?" she asked.

"Nothing," Angel said. "She just lay there. And I thought, 'Don't get involved', and I reversed up, and went out the other way."

Despite her feeling of euphoria, Eva also felt vulnerable and somehow compromised by the discussion of her intimate sexual experiences this morning. And maybe it was this unease which underlay her growing annoyance with the soap opera of Angel's story.

"But isn't that just the problem?" Moana asked, "everyone not getting involved?"

"But this wasn't some old duck who fell over," Angel said defensively. "This was an old duck who went out thinking; 'I'll lie down in front of a car today, and see what happens'." She shivered. "Scary. I could see it in her eyes, when she looked at me."

The phone rang, and Angel moved over to answer it.

Eva found herself re-evaluating their relationship. It seemed somehow different today, like she was more able to view Angel as a person, rather than just in her role as their manager. She was like a kid with big dreams, she thought, and she found that idea scary. The windows had become slightly misted up, and she let her imagination roam over the white shapes on the glass.

Moana waved a hand in front of her face. "You seem spaced," she said.

"I'm high as," Eva admitted.

"What's been happening?"

So much had occurred in such a short time, that Eva found it hard to know what to say, and, finding that this increased the feeling of distance between them, she could make no reply.

"How was that chart stuff?" Moana tried another approach.

"Excellent," Eva told her, finally finding her tongue. The group was really onto something with the astrology, she thought. "I can just go back any time and read it myself."

Seeing that she was getting no where, Moana finally allowed herself to become vulnerable, by revealing an issue of real interest. "Did you end up sleeping with him?"

"In a manner of speaking." Eva smiled shyly. "In my dreams anyway." The memory brought warm feelings. It had been a good night.

"You did it with the machine?" Moana asked incredulously.

Eva nodded.

"That's weird!" she told her.

Eva nodded again. It was weird.

Angel put the phone down. She had obviously been listening to their conversation with one ear, for she turned straight to Eva. "Have you had any more contact with Pearl?" she asked.

"I saw her at breakfast," Eva said.

"How's her attitude?" Moana asked.

Pearl had seemed cold and distant, but confident of the value of her experiences. By contrast Eva sensed insecurity from both the others here in the room, and from Angel also a strong desire to control events, and this contrast was making her re-evaluate her loyalties. "She's letting us go." she admitted.

"She's full of bullshit!" Moana tried to shrug her out of their lives. "It looks like that, then suddenly she's back."

Eva found that she wanted to believe that, but her experience told her otherwise.

"Can't you make her see what she's loosing?" Angel asked her.

Eva was at a loss to know how.

"The other way to go, is to forget her and do the Awards ourselves," Moana jumped in with the suggestion, "then audition a new member when we've got more time."

There was a pause while her idea was absorbed. She had flipped it out, as if you just had to choose, but it seemed like a huge task to Eva. She found it inconceivable that they could actually perform without Pearl, and then she suddenly felt quite depressed as she started coming to terms with not having Pearl there.

Pearl was the power in the trio, and without her energy they wouldn't be the same.

"No, we'll get her back," she found herself saying, although she really couldn't believe it herself.

"I don't think we're at the stage of auditioning yet," Angel agreed. "But maybe we should look at reworking the number for the two of you, just in case."

"I'll have another talk with Pearl," Eva offered. Maybe she could convince her, after all. She had virtually run out of the breakfast, after her ordeal, and didn't know what Pearl was doing. "I don't know what she's up to, today," she admitted. "She gets irritated having me there sometimes, so I have to be careful."

Moana dismissed her suggestion with a shake of her head. "You like going there a bit much," she told her. "I think we should relax a bit on this one."

Perversely this made Eva more inclined to go. "I was going to push her to agree this morning, but I thought I'd give the lawyers a bit more time." It was like she was trying to convince herself, she realised, and she wondered at her own motives.

"They're getting the run-around at the moment," Angel said. "They can't find the right person to talk to in the cult."

Eva felt unable to let go of Pearl, but was so disoriented by her recent experiences, that she couldn't make up her mind what to do.

"I'm working with my Mardigras project today," Moana said, shrugging off any further responsibility.

"We've got that talk show this evening," Angel reminded them, so whatever happens let's meet at the ABC studios at 6pm."

They nodded agreement.

"I'll keep the lawyers onto it today," she said, by way of dismissing them, "and we'll see where we are then."

Eva had been undecided about what to do and, as she closed the front door of the terrace, she sensed that the decision to come home was the wrong one. The place felt stale and empty. There were ash trays and newspapers on the tables, the sink was piled with dirty dishes, and there was a smell from the overflowing rubbish bin. She went into the bathroom, and found no toilet paper, and in her bedroom a pile of clothes which needed folding.

She stayed only long enough to have a shower and change her clothes, and then escaped back to the buzz of the city. She walked aimlessly for some time, down through Darlinghurst, and into Hyde Park. She was beginning to feel a little flat, loosing the certainty of her earlier emotional high, and as this happened her sense of confusion increased. Normally she found that the rhythmic pound of her footsteps was good for sorting out her thoughts, but today she felt no clearer.

She found herself drawn back to the dream-group, as if some clarity might be found there, and she discovered her fingers playing with the visitor card in her pocket. Her feet seemed to find their way back up William Street, to the Cross, without any conscious decision on her part, and it was only as she came to Darlinghurst Road, and was accosted by the human flotsam which was lolling drunkenly on the sidewalk, or standing alluringly in doorways, that she became aware of where she was.

She hesitated when she came to the entrance to the dream-group, and resolved to have a coffee somewhere first, wandering on, past the sickly sweet smells of waffles, and the tourists being accosted by the doormen of the strip joints.

She sat at a cafe by the fountain which sprayed water in the shape of a ball. At the tables about her there were many same-sex couples speaking foreign languages, who were obviously visitors for the Mardigras in a couple of days. The water from the fountain was blowing a fine mist of water toward the cafe, and every now and then it would reach them and cause a stir of exclamation.

She fingered the visitor card again. The main game was Pearl, she reminded herself, and she tried to steel her resolve to convince her to co-operate. It had seemed almost a certainty a few hours ago, but now she felt more vulnerable to rejection.

Eventually she found the resolve to climb the stairs of the dream-group and entered the office. The guy at the desk was someone she didn't know, and she hesitated again.

"Can I help?" he asked.

"I'm Eva," she introduced herself, "Have you seen Pearl recently?"

He shook his head.

This left her nowhere to go, and yet she wanted to look around a little. "Can I book a chart room?" she asked, showing him her card.

He nodded. "Now?"

How perfect, she thought. "Thanks."

He took the card, swiped it through a machine, and gazed at the information which came up on the screen. "You get one more free one," he told her, "then they're $20 a half hour, until you apply for initiation, when they become free again."

She nodded, without really listening to what he was saying.

The glow from the table provided a mellow light in the empty room. She huddled over it, warming herself with the camp-fire of information. Her card had activated the door and the table without a hitch, leaving her a little breathless at the smoothness of her entry.

Now she let her mind play over the lines on the table, and tried to remember what they represented. It just seemed like a mesh of incomprehensible symbols without Matt's guidance. Then she noticed a menu of options around the edge of the table top. One was "symbols as words", and when she touched this each of the planetary symbols, and the symbols for astrological signs, changed to read as the name of that planet or sign.

She recognised Mars and Uranus together. They should be opposite the moon, she thought, and sure enough they were. She noticed that the Sun was also there on the other side of Mars, and she reached out and touched the short line between them.

"Mars together with the Sun denotes a person who is very ambitious," she read, "someone who has a tremendous sexual drive unless it is otherwise channelled." She felt herself blush slightly. "The individual seeks challenge, or always feels challenged."

That was true, she thought. There was also a line between the Sun and the Moon, right across the table. "Sun opposite Moon," read the heading, when she touched it. "This aspect provides a sense of objectivity, as the person must always be aware of others. Obstacles are presented externally, and the individual can feel that the environment, or the people in their life, present barriers to them achieving their goals."

This was linked to another text-box which read; "The orb for this aspect is very wide, which indicates that it will be important for this person to constantly align their forces, and consolidate approaches to life, in order to avoid dissipation. Without a strong relationship between the Sun and the Moon, the sense of purpose of the Sun and the feelings of the Moon do not always work harmoniously together. Their energies must be constantly balanced."

She found it heartening to find a body of knowledge which seemed to give an insight which was consistent with her own experience, and the flux of motion in her life seemed to still for a moment, and she felt an unnatural sense of peace and confidence, an acceptance of the course of her life.

There was a quiet knocking at the door, and she suddenly felt like a naughty child, caught with her hand in the biscuit tin. She made no response, but after a moment it opened anyway, and Matt slid into the room. She felt relieved to see it was him.

"I'm glad I found you," he said, his voice a little crusty with emotion. "They told me you were here. I just wanted to say sorry for this morning." He walked towards her, his movement somehow begging forgiveness.

"It's not your fault," she rushed to his defence. She

194

was surprised how little resentment she felt towards him, and yet part of her was enjoying his humiliation. "But you could have warned me of the consequences of what I was getting involved in," she admonished him. His chest hung forlornly off his shoulders, which empowered her to act out her feelings still further. "Or is it standard practise here to misrepresent things to the newcomers?"

The remark came out of nowhere, but she could tell immediately that she had touched a nerve. She felt that he wanted to agree, and thereby let himself off the hook, but that he couldn't go against the system. He took a deep breath, and put his hands on the side of the table to steady himself. "It doesn't always happen like that," he said. "It's different each time. She just seized on that this morning, for some reason."

There seemed to be some deeper dilemma being played out in him, of which she was only now becoming aware. She had seen hints of it before, she realised however, and maybe this was why she felt no real resentment towards him personally.

"And it doesn't change anything about our feelings for one another," he assured her.

"It does change mine," she told him. "I don't want a relationship which is going to drag my intimate sexual experiences into the spotlight."

He shrugged. "It's not so bad once you get into it. It's quite a cathartic process to talk about your feelings."

195

Maybe he was right, she thought. Perhaps it was just her immaturity which was being uncovered through this experience.

"Do you know where Pearl is?" she asked.

He shook his head.

"Do you think I could convince the leader to support Pearl's involvement in our work?" she suddenly asked him.

He looked at her with an amused expression which should have answered her question.

"Don't you think she would understand the position we're in?" she pursued him.

He shrugged. "I think it's more likely that you will understand the position she's in," he answered enigmatically. "But I might be able to get you a processing session, if you want to try." He had a slightly ambiguous smile, so it wasn't clear who's interests he was serving with the offer.

But although the sense of discomfort she felt from him suggested caution, she felt resolve fire in her guts. This was the breakthrough they needed, she thought. Perhaps she could yet save the day. "When?" she asked.

He pursed his lips. "I'll go and check," he said, and with that the door closed behind him.

18
Processing

Eva found her nerves growing as she waited outside the door to the leader's study. The guard on the door kept looking at her in a weird way, like she was an object, and it made her feel uncomfortable. It had seemed incredibly good luck to get an appointment almost immediately, but the sessions were running late, and she found the palms of her hands growing moist with sweat as she waited. She wiped them on her jeans, and tried to maintain the openness she had felt in the chart room. She was master of her life, she reminded herself.

"I'm glad we had this opportunity," the leader told her, as she was finally ushered into the room. "I've been wanting to talk with you." She was lying back in a black arm chair, and she motioned Eva to another, beside hers. The room was furnished in a traditional manner, the walls were lined with bookshelves, filled with books on astrology and the occult.

Eva sat down. She was busy thinking how to open the conversation, so she didn't have time to wonder why the leader had wanted to talk with her.

"Tell me about your work," the leader encouraged her.

This casual approach put her at ease, and her words started to pour out. "We're working towards the Australasian Song Awards on the weekend," she said. "These things are a bit of a lottery, but if we win, we'll be very well placed to get a good record deal."

The leader nodded encouragingly.

"We're with an independent label for our current single, so hopefully, even if we don't win, there will be good publicity from the Awards." Eva was gaining enthusiasm as she went along. "I think we've actually got quite a good chance of winning, if we can keep it together for another few days." She paused to decide how best to explain their dilemma.

"If you can keep it together?" the leader queried innocently.

Eva nodded. "We have promotional commitments, to be eligible for the awards..." She paused while she considered how to phrase the problem, and then finally just blurted it out. "Since Pearl's been here in the group she's stopped doing these, which is causing us a bit of a problem."

The leader nodded sympathetically.

In a weird disembodied way, Eva registered the outline of her head move between a book entitled *The Pluto Phenomenon*, and another, *The Asteroid Goddesses*, on the wall behind her chair.

"For example, we've got a talk show gig this evening," Eva explained. She felt that the ground had not yet been fully prepared, however she saw the opportunity to make her request, and couldn't resist the urge to do so. "Could you to talk with Pearl, and get her to come to the interview?"

There was a marked change in the leader's attitude at this, and she sat erect. "Doesn't she want to?" she asked.

Eva had assumed that Pearl's attitude was being motivated by the leader, and she became disoriented by her professed lack of involvement. "I haven't asked her," she said haltingly. "But she hasn't been very co-operative lately, and I just thought you might be able to persuade her."

"Oh, I couldn't do that!"

"Why not?" Eva felt a dull ache in her head.

"If I tried to manipulate members in that way, the authorities would be down on me like a pile of rocks."

"I'm just asking you to support her work with us. To allow her the time to fulfil her commitments, and encourage her to do so." She felt that her emotions were too strong for the etiquette of communication, and she sensed she was blowing it.

"I can't be seen to be pushing one way or the other," the leader told her flatly. There was some shouting and some loud bangs from another part of the building, and the muffled noise served to increase the sense of intimacy between them.

Eva suddenly felt desperate. "But it must be good for you to have members who are also high profile members of the community!"

"That depends." The leader looked at her, and for the first time this session Eva felt the power of her contact. "Sometimes too much attention is not a good thing," she explained slowly. "Sometimes members might be too fresh for such an ambassadorial role."

She seemed to be letting Eva into her private thoughts and this built a bond between them, which encouraged Eva to feel felt like she could ask her anything.

"It doesn't seem right that Pearl has given up her property and management rights," she blurted out. "Why do you want to disempower her like that?" She surprised herself with her own directness.

The leader took the challenge in her stride however, and even seemed to welcome it. "I guess it's a question of what you want to do with your life?" she suggested.

"The traditional view is that your property and your career are the stuff of life, but in the group we've moved on from there."

Eva was very focussed on her career, and the leader's comment didn't make any sense.

"You don't spend your time gathering berries and nuts like your ancestors," the leader pointed out to her, "and we've freed ourselves from the individual burden of surviving in the physical world so we can concentrate on issues more related to our own personal development."

It sounded reasonable, and Eva found herself at a loss to know what to say.

"Money weighs us down," the leader told her, "and one of the great benefits of living here is that all financial details are taken care of completely for you. And we do it in bulk, for everyone, so we do it much more efficiently."

It was too reasonable, and Eva felt like she had completely lost her sense of purpose in the interaction.

The leader leaned slightly forward. "But what's this fixation with material success?" she asked quietly.

Eva felt suddenly pressured. "I don't know," she responded, and she felt her breath stick in her throat.

"You have quite an admirable sense of commitment," the leader observed." There was pride in her voice. "But you seem a little too attached to material success, perhaps not letting things take their natural course." Her tone of voice became very disappointed.

This provoked an emotional response in Eva. "I left home when I was sixteen!" she told her sharply. "Then lived on the streets for four years, working with street theatre, which is not the most secure of occupations." There was a tone of righteousness in her own voice.

"Why did you do that?" the leader asked. She appeared genuinely concerned.

Eva was unexpectedly confronted again with her father's death and the break up of her family. She tried to explain what happened, and felt her emotions aroused as she sketched the basic scenario. She still had a lot of unexpressed grief in relation to the break up of her family, she realised.

"Imagine your father were here right now," the leader told her. "What would you say to him?"

She felt the emotion choke in her throat. A thousand little bits of karma jumped to her attention, each demanding the opportunity to be resolved.

"Close your eyes," the leader prompted her, "Just imagine him standing in front of you. He's got a thoughtful expression on his face, and he's not looking at you, but gazing off into the distance. But you know that he can hear when you speak." Her voice had a hypnotic quality. "Just any little thing, it doesn't have to be important."

It was hard to know where to start, however her overwhelming feeling was one of loss. "I miss you Dad," she told him, surprising herself by bursting suddenly into tears. And she did want to say something important, she found, something she had never said to him in real life because their relationship wouldn't allow it.

"I love you Dad," she told him haltingly. "Even though you made it so hard to do that." She felt her emotions surge with the affirmation. It felt like he was actually standing there absolving her of her karma as she spoke, which gave her a wonderful sense of lightness.

"And I forgive you for that time I caught you spying on me in the shower." She could feel the energy burning up the back of her neck. "And for the time you tried to make a pass at me when Mum was away for that week. And I'm sorry I told mum about it, but you know you can't live a lie, and you have to face these things."

She opened her eyes and found the leader nodding approvingly, and sudden became conscious of the fact that she was revealing her intimate family secrets to her.

"Tell your father what you think of him, for doing that," the leader encouraged her.

Eva hesitated. She felt a deep sense of abuse which she hadn't acknowledged, but the love she was feeling for her father felt precious, and she didn't want to destroy this by allowing her anger out.

"Tell the bastard what you think of such despicable behaviour," the leader roared her, her voice suddenly full of righteous indignation.

And the emotion just seemed to well up inside Eva, and overflow. She closed her eyes. "You're a bastard to try to take advantage of me that way. And I hate you for abusing my faith in you. You fat, small-minded pervert!" She started shaking uncontrollably. "And it's just lucky for you that I had the sense to run away."

The leader moved over to sit on the arm of her chair, and rested a hand on her shoulder. Eva opened her eyes and looked up, directly into her eyes. There were no barriers between them, and the contact was deep and intimate.

"These things take time to resolve," the leader said. "You understand that don't you?"

Eva nodded, without really knowing why, and she felt helpless and disoriented.

"But this is the way we can process these experiences," the leader said, "and simply by bringing them up they become resolved." She pulled Eva toward her, and she found herself snuggling down on the woman's lap like a child, and felt her stroking her hair.

"You're such a good little baby," the leader told her, soothing away Eva's cares with her fingers. "You try so hard to look after everyone." Eva felt totally disorientated by the turn of events, but the stroking fingers settled her emotions.

"I don't want you to think any more," the leader said, "just let your mind go blank, and I'm going to tell you a

204

story that might help explain what's happening."

Eva felt as if the voice was coming from far away.

"This is a story about women, and their place in the world. Because this is changing, and not just changing so that women are becoming equal to men, but we are slowly developing a matriarchal society."

Despite her relaxed state, Eva felt an anxious sweat on her forehead, and she wiped it with her sleeve.

"Women will inevitably take the dominant role in the future because we are better communicators, which is becoming more and more important in the information age." Her voice paused, but her fingers kept moving.

"And we're starting it here in the group. This is the birth of a real new world order, and you can participate by joining us." Again the pause of the voice. It had a real hypnotic effect.

"This is what Pearl has discovered, and why she prefers it, to the glamour of your music industry."

Eva wanted to protest, but couldn't raise the energy to do so.

"But to embrace the new order you have to give up your petty ambitions, which just lock you into the pattern of your existing life, and reinforces your subservience. You have to learn how to be an effective member of a community. How to be sensitive to others, and yet take the lead when required. But first you need to strip away all of that person you used to be, the limited you, so the new you can evolve."

Eva was drifting in her mind.

The leader lifted her head, so she could stand, and return to her chair. "That's what Pearl is doing," she said, holding Eva's eye contact. "Do you think you would be up to that challenge?"

Eva found she couldn't answer the question, although she wanted to say yes, as she sensed this was the response the leader wanted.

"Come to the Pluto Encounter tonight," the leader suggested, "and you'll get a bit more of an insight." Her eyes twinkled for the first time.

Eva found herself nodding.

She felt high, but completely disoriented, by the time she found herself back out in the corridor. The guard still had that weird look, and she hurried along to the office and asked after Pearl, but no-one knew where she was. That left her at a loss to know what to do.

"Are you coming to the encounter tonight?" the guy asked her.

She looked blankly at him.

"The Pluto encounter, tonight."

She nodded, then shrugged. "I'll see." She felt too confused to know what was happening, and was not even together enough to leave a message for Pearl, before heading out into the street.

She picked her way through the Cross, and let her feet pound along Victoria Street, and down the stairs to Woolloomooloo. They took her past the Naval base, and in through the Botanical Gardens to Circular Quay.

She registered very little more than the sensations about her as she walked, her mind seemingly unable to hold images or thoughts in any coherent form. She was just letting her feet have their head, and pounding out some of the confusion of her life.

She rounded a corner in the gardens, and a vista of flowers opened in the tinted light of the evening. Her feelings blossomed at the sight. On a bench a little further on lay an old man with no shoes and dirty feet. "Women are better communicators," she heard the leader's voice, and she had a vision of men everywhere lying derelict on park benches, which made her laugh. The man snorted in his sleep, and she hurried on.

It wasn't until she reached Circular Quay that she thought about the talk show again, and realised she was already late herself.

She stood leaning against a rail, gazing at the harbour for an eternity, as she agonised over what to do. She felt far too vulnerable to brave the inane scrutiny of the public, and yet her sense of responsibility demanded that she fulfil her commitments.

She found herself unable to make a decision one way or the other, until finally she summoned up the will to take charge of her life and brave the talk show, only to look at her watch and discover that it was already too late. She felt like a failure for not being there to support Moana, and she found a seat at a cafe, and ordered a hot chocolate, and some garlic bread, to try and settle her feelings.

On the wall was the poster for the Song Awards. The image seemed to mock her, and she felt an empty vulnerability, as if everything were falling to pieces around her.

She was having the occasional flash-back to the session with the leader. And, every now and then, the memory of the guy in the office would ask, "Are you coming to the encounter tonight?"

A bag-lady rummaged in the rubbish bin beside her. She was a short woman, barely taller than the bin itself, and she was using a stick to poke through the refuse. She pulled out a can of coke and, shaking the last drips from it, placed it down on the pavement and crushed it with one smooth motion of her foot. Then she tossed it in a bulging canvas bag which she was dragging along beside her.

Eva took a sip of her chocolate, it was already getting cold, and she gulped down some more. The sweetness spread through her, and with it came a sense of acceptance. Her life stood in relief against that of the bag-lady, and although it seemed chaotic and out of control, it was still rich with experience and potential.

A young man in tight jeans and no shirt, loitered near the cafe. He looked incongruous in the evening light, his well built chest blatantly sexual in this unusual context. He had a tatty donation tin in his hand.

"For the handicapped," he told her, the lights from the ferries playing on his skin.

She looked at him, and whether it was her current state of mind, or perhaps her insight was accurate, but he looked like a real con artist, and she just waved him on.

It was hard to tell what was real any more.

It was quite a bit later that she started thinking again about the prospect of facing Moana when she got home. Not only had she not been able to get Pearl to the talk show, but she hadn't even been able to make it herself, and she felt ashamed of her failure.

She didn't want to confront her friend and, the more she thought about it, the more attractive the Pluto encounter sounded. There was something about the evenings at the group which excited her, some sort of heightened sense of reality, where the tried conventions of everyday life weren't necessary, or accepted. In a sense it seemed more real, and in a funny way safer, than her own crazy life.

Pluto Encounter

The beat of music already began to entice Eva as she climbed the stairs of the Dream group. She felt the rhythm in her bones.

A female guard stopped her at the top of the stairs. "It's a private session tonight," she explained. "Have you got a card?"

Eva went to shake her head, and then remembered the visitors card for the chart equipment. "Will this do?" she asked, producing it out of her pocket.

"Try it in there." She motioned to a machine on the table, and Eva placed it in the slot and dragged it towards her. A green light glowed, and her details came up on the view-screen. The guard motioned her past. "You're okay," she told her.

Eva wondered why the special deal tonight, as she was drawn by the music along the hall and into the studio. The atmosphere was highly charged. Tables and chairs were arranged, cafe style, against the curtained-off cubicles, leaving the middle of the room free for dancing. Above everyone the video screen held a visual of mission control, with one corner of the screen following the probe's progress as it approached the planet.

Eva stood just inside the door. She couldn't see anyone she knew, and she began to wonder whether it had been wise to come. She thought again of Moana, and imagined her sitting at home wondering what had happened, and felt another twinge of guilt.

A young guy appeared beside her. "Hi," he said.

"Hi," she responded.

"Have I seen you here before?" he asked.

She smiled. "I've been hanging around a bit." She had noticed him at one of the meals. He was somewhere up in the organisation.

"You're Pearl's friend, aren't you?" he said, recalling something. "You sing together."

Eva nodded. "Have you seen her tonight?"

"She's here somewhere." He looked towards the dance floor, without sighting her. "You want to dance?" he asked, turning back to her.

She paused. He seemed to be a bit too keen, but the pulsing movement was definitely attracting her. "Okay," she said, surprising herself.

As she approached the dance floor she felt the

rhythm roll over her, and she released her body to its influence. Soon she was no longer aware of the guy, and she allowed the flow of the interactions that naturally spring up between people when they're dancing.

She picked up on people's movements and played with them, savouring the emotion and attitude which had brought each moment of physical expression to life, and then bounce it back to it's owner in a new form.

One after another however, the guys started coming on to her, and she found herself slowly working her way across the dance floor to escape.

Finally she spotted Matt huddled over some equipment on a table below the video screen, and, breaking from the dance mass, she went over.

He had his back to her as she approached, and she touched him lightly on the shoulder, and then ran her hand down his back.

Without looking up, he reached out and returned the caress, and his touch felt light and playful on the loose fitting cloth of her pants. Then he turned, and for a moment they looked one another in the eye, and then hugged. Eva gave herself over to it, as she had to the rhythm of the dancing, and Matt allowed their contact to grow more and more intimate, without a hint of the reserve which he had been adopting lately. She needed the physical contact, and for an eternal moment she felt relaxed and at peace.

Then, brushing her forehead with his lips, he pulled away from her. "I've got to rig this equipment before the flypast," he explained, his voice sounding a little crusty. "I've only got half an hour."

She nodded. She noticed that there was a small raised stage area below the video screen, which was covered in black plastic sheets, taped together at the joints. The plastic extended right up the wall at the sides of the stage, and the back was lined with rows of red buckets. She wondered what it was.

The equipment on which he was working seemed to be connected with a lighting show, so she guessed that it all must be part of the performance in which Pearl was going to be involved.

Her eyes panned about the room, searching for her friend, however without success.

"Are you staying for the encounter?" he asked.

She nodded again. He represented her most comfortable point of contact with this piece of the puzzle of her reality, and now that she had found him, she was loath to return to the meat market on the dance floor.

"You're welcome to sit here if you want to," he said, sensing how she felt, and motioning to a couple of chairs beside the equipment table.

She touched him lightly on the cheek to thank him,

and sat down.

"How was the Processing?" he asked.

She shuddered. "Not what I expected." She felt a great reluctance to talk about the session. She felt like a little kid who had broken a petty family taboo, and as she awaited discovery the magnitude of the transgression was blown up, out of all proportion, in her mind. She realised this was because the leader now knew one of her inner emotional secrets, and this made her feel vulnerable.

"Often it's not easy to face the stuff that comes up," he suggested.

He was testing the waters, and at first she just nodded agreement, but then this response stuck in her throat. "But what good does it do to bring them up anyway?" she demanded.

He looked startled by the question. "Healing the wounds," he suggested.

"Opening the wounds maybe," she responded. "Is there any treatment?"

He seemed unable to hide his own unease. "But I think it is simply valuable to bring these things up, and so release them," he said, his tone was defensive.

She nodded. Maybe he was right.

"I guess you can't agree with everything," he suddenly admitted. "You have to say on balance that it's going the right way." He seemed surprisingly challenged by her comments, which gave her a glimpse behind the confident person, who was important for his skills, to the agonising which seemed to be going on inside. She reached out her hand to rub his arm, and reassure him.

A voice started intoning a count-down, and Matt jumped to cut the music. There was a hiss of static, and the visual of mission control gave way to the perspective of the probes, as the bodies stopped moving on the dance floor, and everyone's attention was drawn up to the screen, and then sucked out into space together with the improbably small machines with which they were seeking to explore the majesty of the universe.

Eva noticed the leader enter the room, and walk in a slow ritual manner towards the stage. She was followed, several paces behind, by Pearl, who was wearing a white bath robe, and Eva felt her heartbeat increase at the sight of her friend. Four other people, all in single file, and each wearing similar robes, followed her.

Pearl took up a position standing motionless in the middle of the plastic covered stage, and the others lined up at the side, while the leader stirred the buckets behind. Everyone in the room was sitting collapsed onto the floor where they had been dancing, or lying propped up on one another, as the visual of the approaching planet filled them all with awe.

Eva discovered a mysterious bright spot which seemed to rotate with Pluto. The surface of the planet looked shiny, like it was covered with ice, so maybe it was a reflection, she reasoned. The camera panned from the planet, past the twin probe, and back towards the sun. From this distance she found it was impossible to see the earth, and the sun itself was only a very bright star.

The camera panned back to the looming planet, and Matt punched in a tape of some drumming, and slowly wound up the volume behind the sounds of the probe's communication. The tribal rhythm seemed appropriate to the event, and as the beat reached a climax, Pearl suddenly dropped her robe. She was naked underneath, and Eva felt her heart jump at the discovery.

Matt turned on a laser machine. producing a fine point of light which cut across the stage area. He tried to adjust the settings on the desktop to shape the beam to her body. He was still learning to operate it however, and his beam was crossing the lines of her body like the scribble of a young child with a new colouring book.

He became quickly exasperated, and his helplessness seemed so comic that Eva giggled despite her shock. Then he gave up, and pulled down the volume of the drumming.

Pearl started to hum. The leader picked up a bucket and gave it to one of the other performers, who approached Pearl. There was a moment of tension as he reached into it, and then he pulled out a handful of green paint and daubed it on her naked chest.

Eva felt the sensation of the material as if on her own skin, and she felt acutely uncomfortable for her friend.

One at a time, the other performers also took a bucket of paint from the leader and daubed Pearl with various colours. There was something eternal in both the ritual on stage, and the inevitable approach of the planet above them. However Eva sat poised, watching Pearl like a cat eyeing a bird. One wrong move and she'd spring to the rescue. However exactly what she would do, she couldn't actually imagine. And exactly what would constitute a wrong move, also became harder and harder to decipher.

As each performer finished, they walked back to the leader, who took their bucket and gave them a new one. Pearl was humming quietly throughout this process.

Then she lay down on her back on the plastic, as the first figure approached for the second time. She took an egg out of her bucket and cracked it from some height over Pearl's chest. The yoke broke as it hit her body, and the liquid splattered over her tits.

This was getting sick, Eva thought, and she felt her stomach turn. The next figure had a bottle of oil which he poured liberally up and down Pearl's whole body. The next had tomato sauce, and then came flour, grass clippings, margarine, and so it went on and on.

Eva thought again of Moana, and she felt an overwhelming desire to run home, and leave this strange experience. It was too weird, but somehow she couldn't move.

One of the men disrobed and lay down in front of Pearl, and the procedure was repeated with him, and then with each of the others, in ritual fashion, as the planet swung past on the video screen above them.

"I don't feel good," Eva told Matt.

He was fine tuning the video image, and he simply looked at her and smiled encouragingly, as if everything were perfectly normal. Coupled with her growing sense of unexpressed unease from him, this response gave the event a very surreal tinge, which seemed to turn it into an art event, rather than a real life experience.

Pluto's moon came into view, dominating the planet's skyline like a vast football.

All six figures were lying covered with material, and the leader had completed the last slops of the buckets onto them. Matt faded up a music sound-track, and the bodies on stage began to slither and slide, and wallow in the material, with the laser light picking out a physical feature here and there in the mud bath.

Eva felt a revulsion at the spectacle, and at the same

time strangely liberated by the breaking of taboos about intimacy, and about making a mess. However the animal nature of the ritual seemed to call up the shadowy side of the participants, and she found this reflected in each of the faces in the audience, and it sent a shiver down her spine.

She felt her life somehow twist inside out, as the probes pivoted around the gravitational pull of Pluto above them, and Pearl participated in the encounter ritual. It was like shedding a skin, and things could never be the same again.

On the dance floor, a great deal of physical petting and cuddling was occurring, stimulated by the release on stage.

Matt moved his chair closer to hers, and she rested her head on his shoulder. He stroked her forehead. In an environment stalked by shadows, he alone seemed at peace with himself, and she valued their contact.

She had a sense of her life as if broken into pieces, like a disassembled jigsaw puzzle, and now she would have to put it back together in a new way. She resolved take things quietly for the next few days.

She was conscious of the rich majesty of the canopy of stars above them, as Matt walked her home in the early hours. Even with the background light from the city, the stars still shone out across vast stretches of space to light each fragile moment of their lives.

Matt had been trying to convince her to stay in the group overnight, but she had felt such a strong need to be on familiar territory, that she had convinced him to walk home with her. She clung to his arm as they walked. Despite its bizarre nature, the encounter ritual had aroused her sexually, and she was conscious of a strong desire to make love with him.

"You could spend the night with me," she suggested, "and go back in the morning."

He shook his head. "You know I can't."

"Just stay for an hour," she teased him. "No-one would know."

"I'd know," he said. "I'm not good with secrets."

They paced on in silence, but she sensed that he was still considering it. His arm, around her waist, pulled her closer as they walked, and the gesture forced them to be more sensitive to one-another's rhythm.

Eva was experiencing her physical sensations in a richer way than normal, and she concentrated on these, as they covered the last stretch home.

They discovered Moana reading by candle-light on the couch, and their entrance seemed to disturb the somewhat thick atmosphere in the room. Eva noticed two beer bottles lying empty on the floor beside the couch.

Moana looked at her, and Eva felt herself pinned to the spot by her gaze. Moana coolly and relentlessly assessed her, and Eva waited, standing hand in hand with Matt, for a signal on how to proceed. She hadn't prepared herself for this interaction, and she felt both guilty for her self obsession, and unable to express how much she had personally been risking over the past couple of days. In this dilemma she discovered a deep well of self pity, which she tittered precariously on the edge of for some moments, as the emotional currents surged strongly about them in the half light.

Moana just stared however, offering no release from the experience, and after a while Eva felt Matt's fingers attempting to caress hers into action. Moana hadn't acknowledged him, and Eva felt unable to proceed without her approval. Finally, to break the trance, Matt simply turned to go, and Eva followed him back to the door.

"I'm sorry," she said.

"Don't be," he told her, "it's better this way."

They kissed goodbye. His lips were hungry, and they seemed to stand like that for ages, leading her to believe that they might yet make it into bed together, but finally he pulled away.

"I don't think you should come to the group for a while," he told her suddenly, the comment surprisingly echoing her own as yet unarticulated feelings. She would have expected the opposite counsel from him however, and she wondered what had motivated this change of heart.

"It's not good for you," he told her, answering her unexpressed question. "I can't explain why now, but just stay away, and I'll give you a call."

She nodded, a little stunned by his change of allegiance.

"See you soon," he said, and she watched him fade into the night.

"What happened to you?" Moana demanded, as Eva re-entered the lounge. There was a clear edge of emotion in her voice.

Eva raised her arms in helplessness, how could she start to explain her day?

"How come you didn't turn up at the ABC?" Moana persisted, and the fire of emotions, which she had been suppressing while Matt was there, rose up into her eyes and her face.

Eva had no sensible answer, and in her frustration and helplessness, she burst into tears.

"Yeah, that's an easy way out, aint it?" Moana taunted her.

Eva wanted to run upstairs to her room. However she

made herself walk to the table and sit down, and then buried her head in her arms. "I can't keep track of it any more," she sobbed. "I can't work out what's happening."

There was a pause.

"Maybe we should leave it till the morning," Moana said. Her voice suddenly sounded flat, and Eva looked up to see that the anger had washed out of her. She stood and came over to the table. "I'm sorry, I guess you've had a hard day."

Eva reached out to pull her closer, and rested her head against her friend's warm stomach. Moana started stroking her hair, and Eva relaxed with the soothing touch of her fingers.

She could hear the soft gurgling sounds of her friend's body, and through this she felt the life energy of which they were all manifestations. This feeling was strong and vital, and through it she sensed that she could relax and allow the flow of her growth.

20

Shifting Ground

When she awoke the next morning, the sunlight was already streaming into the room. Moana was asleep beside her, and Eva snuggled closer to her warm body.

She lay dozing, allowing dream images to move in and out of her consciousness, mixed with sensations of the smell and texture of Moana's hair.

In one dream, she found herself water-skiing, as she had once as a child. The boat was going fast, and she could only hold on desperately to the rope as she bounced from wave to wave. She had a sense that if she let go and fell, she'd be hurt, and might be lost forever, and so she hung on grimly.

Inevitably, after a time, she did fall, but as she hit the water, she seemed to simply bounce along the surface. There was no sensation cold or wet, just the pleasure at being able to finally let go and relax.

She played with the sliding movement, first on her stomach, and then on her back. Then something tickled her mind, and she awoke again, sweating, whether from the exertion of the dreams, or the warmth of the sun in the room, she wasn't certain.

Moana was now up, and Eva climbed straight into the shower, and let the water clean the sweat from her spirit.

The sweet taste of dried fruit, and crisp crunch of nuts, mingled delightfully in Eva's mouth. She added a little yoghurt to her bowl. Moana was sitting opposite, with the morning paper, and Eva watched the little flickers of emotion in her face as she read.

"I want to stay home today," Eva suddenly told her friend.

Moana looked up.

"I need to nurture myself a little," she explained.

"Angel wants to see us."

The world outside seemed big and oppressive. "Can't she come here?" Eva was surprised by the sharp edge in her voice.

"Maybe." Moana shrugged.

A slight breeze, from the open french doors behind her, rustled the pages of her paper, and the sound slowly settling Eva's ruffled emotions. "Maybe we could even do it tomorrow," she found herself suggesting.

Moana was wearing a night robe which hung open at the front, revealing her small brown breasts. They hadn't made love last night, just sought the comfort of each other's bodies, but Eva now found herself attracted to her friend physically, and the sensation confused her.

Moana shrugged, and her robe adjusted with the movement to cover her chest. "You getting your period?" she asked.

Eva shook her head. "Should be another couple of weeks."

Her friend thought for a moment. "I'll give Angel a call," she offered. "Y'know the rehearsal is tomorrow?"

She seemed half teasing in her tone, however Eva felt a sudden desperation at this realisation. "Are the Awards the next day?"

Moana nodded. "Same as Mardigras."

It seemed impossible to get it together either way in that time, and Eva released herself again to the seemingly inevitable flow of events. She sighed. "I just know we'll miss her," she said, and in her mind she saw Pearl entering stage and watched her feet start to move. "She can always just turn it on."

Moana nodded. "You never know with Pearl," she said mysteriously.

Eva struggled to understand what she meant. "How's

that?" she asked.

"When we get in front of that crowd," she predicted, "I bet she's there, getting her piece of the action."

Eva felt surprised by her attitude, and it made her doubt her own instincts in the matter.

"She's a sucker for the big crowds," Moana explained. "And anyway, Angel's got the goods on them." She raised her arms.

Eva wasn't so certain any longer, and she longed to have Moana's apparent equanimity.

"How weird." Angel's comment echoed Moana's facial expression, as Eva tried to explain about the Pluto ritual. It was hard to put the experience into words, and it seemed far fetched in the light of day.

"Everyone sat and watched?" Moana asked. "Like performance art?"

Eva nodded. "At first," she agreed. She felt hesitant about discussing sexuality openly, and she paused and swallowed. "However after a while people were getting turned on, and they started petting, and cuddling one another." A shudder ran down her spine as relating the memory released the awkwardness she had felt.

"Where?" Angel asked.

"On the floor mostly," Eva laughed.

"Were you okay?" Moana asked.

Eva welcomed the concern in her voice. She nodded. "I was with Matt."

"Petting and cuddling on the floor?" Moana enquired. There was a slight edge to her voice. Eva caught her eye, and they shared an embarrassed smile at discovering themselves in this situation.

"Yes," Eva admitted, thankful that she hadn't told her about the virtual swap.

Angel was looking from one to the other, trying to discern what was going on between them. "I think it's best if we try and keep our relationships on a professional level," she said, more to Moana than Eva. She seemed to be echoing an earlier conversation, and Moana nodded, and the communication lapsed as Moana made no further response.

"I had a session with the leader," Eva told them. She felt like she was confessing this reluctantly, but was also proud of her courage. "Trying to convince her to help us."

Moana seemed to look deep within her for a moment. "Any luck?" she asked off-handedly, and Eva felt a laugh well up from deep inside at the irony of the question, and it bubbled out a little hysterically as she shook her head.

"It appears we need to show them we're serious," Angel decided. She stood up, as if to go and do just that. "We'll file an entrapment suit," she explained. "It just costs us to prepare the documents at this stage. And the safe bet is that they won't want the publicity, and will try and settle with us out of court."

Eva felt something catch in her throat at the suggestion. However it felt like more than she could do to look after herself at the moment, and she knew she had to release Pearl to her own fate. "I just hope we're not loosing sight of Pearl in all this," she repeated, almost to herself.

The shit was about to hit the fan, she could feel it building. She was trying to read, but Moana had the television playing, as she worked on her Mardigras costume, and Eva found the noise disturbing. She decided to go out to the garden, and stood up to do so, when her attention was caught by a news-flash.

"In a sensational development just to hand," the woman newsreader announced, "the management of one of the contestants in the Australasian Song Awards, the Dance Sisters, an all female trio, has just filed a suit in the civil court claiming entrapment and psychological abuse of one of the members, by a cult known as the Dream-group, which is based in Kings Cross."

Moana had also stopped what she was doing and she stood open-mouthed in front of the screen, her hair and shirt dotted with threads, feathers, and scraps of material.

"The Dream-group are reportedly a cult, engaged in

group sex, emotional manipulation, and the brain-washing of members, under the guise of therapy." The woman news reader was coming to the end of the item, and her voice brightened, despite the bizarre topic. "More on this, and other stories in the news at six."

Eva couldn't believe she was actually part of this story, or even that confronting them so publicly was a sensible thing to do.

"Want a drink?" Moana called, standing in the open french doors.

Eva nodded from the garden chair. "A sweet tea please," she said. The weather was blessing them with sun today, and she was making the most of it.

The phone rang and she heard Moana answer it. The rush and roar of the city beyond the bamboo, drowned out the conversation inside, but somehow she guessed who it was and she found herself trying to hide in the flood of sense perceptions from the afternoon.

"It's Matt," Moana called out, and Eva sighed at the accuracy of her intuition. She found herself anticipating some weird invitation as she walked inside, and caught herself rehearsing refusals, before reminded herself to let go of her expectations as she picked up the handset.

"Hi Matt."

"I thought I might come over," he said.

"Did you?" She felt a rush of pleasure and surprise. "When?"

"Now."

"What for?"

"The leader wants me to sort this entrapment thing out with you," he said.

Things were moving quicker than she could grasp, but in a funny way she felt disappointed that was why he was coming.

"I've also got something else I need to say to you in private," he added in a whisper, and she felt his emotions welling up on the other end of the phone.

"Okay," she agreed. "Stay there and I'll call Angel to make a time." She pressed recall to put him on hold, and then stood there, absorbing the interaction, the phone handset hanging in her hand. She felt a sudden hope that it might all come together, a feeling which she quickly pushed aside, in case it was disappointed. There was a sound of the toilet flushing upstairs. It was like she was in shock, she thought, and she dialled Angel's number, and listened to it ring.

There was a commotion from the living room, and the sound awoke Eva out of her day dreams in the garden. Angel appeared at the french doors, followed by Moana, wearing a feather head-dress, and very little else.

"Is that your costume?" Eva asked, giggling.

Moana grinned at her own daring, then rose onto her tiptoes and pranced across the patio as if it were a catwalk. They applauded, and she repeated the movement back towards the doors, then disappeared into the house with a final toss of her head and a flick of her foot.

Angel looked at Eva, and they shared a smile at her exhibitionism.

Angel tapped her nose knowingly. "Seems they do want to make a deal." She walked over and tousled Eva's hair. "How are you managing?"

She smiled ruefully. "I'm a little fragile at the moment."

Eva answered the door, and found Pearl and Matt standing on the step. It felt somehow disturbing to see them standing there like a couple, and any hopes Eva might have cherished were dashed by one look at Pearl's face. She was expecting a fight, her eyes were fixed and wide, and she pushed straight past with little more than a glance of acknowledgement.

Matt stood motionless for a moment. He looked as if he wanted to say something, but couldn't find the words, and this effort gave his face a strange stiffness.

She rubbed his arm to reassure him, and again it felt like he was about to say something, and then Moana called out from the next room.

"Are you guy's coming?" she demanded.

Eva pulled him inside, closed the door behind him, and ushered him though into the living room. The atmosphere felt difficult as they joined the others around the coffee table. Angel was standing by the fireplace, with Moana sitting on one couch, facing Pearl on the other.

Pearl sat alert and unnaturally motionless. "I feel like a pawn in this game," she announced, without ceremony.

Angel shook her head. "You're definitely a main player."

"I feel like I'm being bartered off to keep the peace between two warring clans," she responded, which gave Eva the impression that she had been instructed to come to meet them, against her own wishes.

"That's the last thing we want," she told Pearl, as she collapsed on the couch beside Moana. Pearl looked at her in a way which held no warmth whatsoever. Her eyes felt like those of a cornered animal, and Eva tried to reassure her with her own love.

Matt sat down beside Pearl. He put his hand on her shoulder to support her, and she softened at the contact, and rested her forehead on his hand for a moment. Eva found the intimacy between them bothered her, and she suddenly felt the need to pull back emotionally from them both.

Moana pulled her feet up and lay back against the cushions. Eva felt her friend's toes teasing at her ribs. She tried to brush her foot away, but Moana was wearing a mischievous expression, and Eva had to grab her ankle to subdue her. She could feel Moana's muscles rippling under her skin, and she registered Matt's apparent discomfort at their rough and tumble. She grinned at him. It went both ways, she realised.

"We just want you to pull your weight," Moana suddenly challenged Pearl, and they eyed one another like cats.

"We're offering a deal," Angel jumped in quickly, as if dealing with squabbling children. "You do the song awards, and we'll absolve you from the rest of the stuff."

This was the first Eva had heard of it, and the compromise seemed only to confirm the collapse of her long term dreams for the trio.

"The promos and television gigs if we win?" Pearl asked.

Angel shrugged. "Just do the awards and we're happy."

"What about the rehearsal tomorrow?" Pearl pressed her.

"We obviously need you there."

Pearl looked at their manager for a long time. Then she looked at Matt. It wasn't only her pride which was in the way, Eva realised. She seemed to be seeking guidance from him, in a way which Eva had never seen her do with anyone else. It was as if she wasn't fully able to make her own decisions any longer.

This was what Eva feared more than anything.

Matt seemed to have a calming effect on her however, and he nodded imperceptibly in response to her unspoken question.

"Okay," Pearl finally agreed. "Just to get this over with as quickly as possible."

Eva couldn't believe it, but her instincts were working faster than her logical mind. "What about that thing I signed?" she asked. "I want that stopped as part of this deal." Her eye contact challenged either Pearl or Matt to admit their betrayal, but she sensed instead a guarded reserve, which had the same effect.

"Naturally," Angel said, in her support. "We'll also need something in writing."

Pearl and Matt looked at one another. Neither seemed keen to accept responsibility, and Matt stole an awkward glance towards Eva.

"I think we better take it back to the group for a decision," he said.

"You better ring and check," Pearl told him, and he stood and walked to the phone.

They were different people when they were together. They seemed more on their guard, as if aware that any comments would be carried back to the group.

Matt stood transfixed in front of Eva on the doorstep. He hadn't had an opportunity to talk with her alone, but obviously didn't want to explain this in front of Pearl.

"Are you coming?" Pearl asked him, turning back as she came to the edge of the curb. She had been embarrassed by having to take the decision back to the group, and she just wanted to leave.

Eva found herself experiencing the day in fragments, and she felt tired from the effort of linking them together. The emotional drag felt visible in the darkness around them as Matt seemed unable to move.

"I'll see you later," she told him, and she kissed him on the lips. His were soft and moist, and she caressed them with her tongue. Then she pulled back and looked at him. The quiet seething which she sensed inside him, reflected her own inner turmoil.

"I think it may be best that we stop seeing one another for a while," she told him, feeling proud of the openness to change which this statement represented.

He shook his head. "I'll call you," he whispered, and he turned and followed Pearl over to a car with the words; 'Dare to Dream' airbrushed on the side.

Eva watched them go, and while part of her wanted to go with them and loose herself in their experiences, another part desperately needed time for reflection, and she savoured the poignancy of the moment as she watched the car disappear.

21

Surprise Decision

Eva was curled up with her book that evening on the couch, burrowed into the cushions, when the phone rang. Moana had just had a bath and was standing beside the table, but she ignored the ringing, picked up the remote control for the television instead, and came over to sit beside Eva. As a result the answering machine took the call, but the caller didn't leave a message.

Moana started flicking through the channels with the sound down. She was wrapped in a large white towel which made her brown limbs and neck look like chocolate icing. Her left hand was resting on Eva's foot, and after a time her thumb started rubbing gently into the soft part, behind the toes. Eva's whole body seemed to melt at the touch, and sensing her pleasure, Moana put down the remote and picked up the foot in both hands.

Eva put down the book, and allowed the television images, and the physical sensations to occupy her attention in a chaotic but comforting sort of way.

The phone rang again, and they looked at one another. Neither wanted to take it, and the machine took the call promptly this time, however again there was no message.

Eva began to wonder if it might be Matt. She felt as if she were in a kind of limbo; despite the agreement which they had hopefully reached, key emotional issues remained unresolved, and the long term dream still seemed shattered. As long as she didn't dwell on these things however, everything seemed to proceed as usual.

Moana put her foot down, and Eva leaned towards her, rubbed her head gently against her friend's, and enjoyed the sensation of her short strands of hair brushing against Moana's wiry cushion.

The phone rang again, and, summoning up reserves of decisiveness which surprised her, she kissed Moana on the cheek, and just reached it before the machine.

"Eva."

"It's Matt."

"I guessed it," she told him. "Are you scared of answering machines?"

"I've got to talk to you," he told her, ignoring her teasing.

"When?"

240

"Now."

"I thought we were going to have some space?" Her heart was beating.

"I've just got to talk to you," he repeated, and there was a real urgency in his voice.

She felt confused, and looked over at Moana for advice, as if she might be intuiting his suggestion.

"I've also got some information you may find useful," he added mysteriously, "But I can't talk about it now."

Moana was shaking her head.

"He's got some information for us," Eva told her, and her friend's gesture changed in mid-shake to a nodding motion. But it was the urgency in Matt's voice which really persuaded her.

"Okay, see you soon," she told him. There were small beads of sweat on her brow, as she put the phone down, however she sensed that possibly some of the real issues were now going to be addressed, and it gave her a funny sense of hope.

There was a soft but insistent tapping on the door, which could only just be heard in living room, and Eva went and unlocked it.

Matt stepped inside as if evading pursuit.

"What's up?" she demanded.

He motioned her to be quiet until he had closed and

locked the door, and then, without a word, he put his arms around her waist and pulled her to him.

His forward behaviour overwhelmed her reserve, and, as their lips met, she closed her eyes and released herself to the embrace. Something had changed between them.

Then he pulled back, and she opened her eyes, to find his gazing back at her with an unsettling closeness.

"I'm moving out," he announced.

She felt a rush of surprise and pleasure at the news, coupled with a waft of the emotional turmoil which must have preceded his decision. "Just so that we can make love, right?" she teased him, now suddenly a little apprehensive at the prospect.

"Not solely." He grinned, but then his brave face seemed to dissolve to reveal the trials which had brought him to this point. "It's been building up."

Her heart went out to him, and she felt a surge of strength as a result of his decision. Everything had seemed to be falling apart, and now, through the cracks in her former self, new energy was flowing back. She took him by the hand and led him into the living room.

Moana studied them impassively.

From a little dart of her eyes however, Eva could tell that their holding hands disturbed her, and she released his grip, in deference to her friend's feelings.

Matt sat on the second couch. "I've got something

which should provide a good insurance policy for me, and may be useful to you in your negotiations over Pearl." He reached into his pocket, and produced a piece of paper. Little beads of sweat had broken out on his forehead.

"Why do you need an insurance policy?" Eva asked. It didn't sound good.

"I know how they work." He looked at her. "I have a lot of information which could harm them." He left it hanging as to exactly what that could mean, but the implication worried her.

Moana reached out her hand, and he gave her the piece of paper. Eva moved around to look over her shoulder as she read what looked like a list of tax information.

"What is it?" Moana asked.

"A file of investments about which the tax department knows nothing," he told them.

She whistled. "There's a lot of money here."

He nodded. "There's a lot at the leader's disposal, which doesn't get accounted for publicly."

Eva sat beside him. She rested her arm on the back of the couch and lightly rubbed his back. All the seductive foreplay over the past week had enmeshed her, and now that the impediment to the consummation of their relationship had disappeared, she felt the pull of it strongly.

Moana stood, and paced restlessly. She was excited.

"Why are you moving out?" Eva couldn't help inquiring.

"Many reasons." He sighed. "It's hard to explain."

She stroked her fingers through his hair. He seemed unable to explain himself, and it felt like she was staring into a deep well.

"We should really do a virtual-link," he suddenly said, "then I could show you the pressure you come under." He wiped his forehead with his sleeve.

"Aren't they forbidden?" Eva asked, remembering something that Pearl had told her.

He nodded. "But we could just go and do it." The rustle of the city about them seemed to seep in through the walls. "Later tonight, no-one would know."

It felt to Eva like the lure of the cookie jar, while the parents are out.

Moana looked suddenly suspicious. "Is that like you did the other night?" she asked.

He shook his head. "You're thinking of the swap," he told her, "which is virtual sex." He laughed, and suddenly his former energy was back. "I'm not suggesting that."

"So what are you suggesting?"

"A link," he said. "Where we do a virtual journey together."

"How does that work?" Moana was determined to

understand what he was proposing.

"I have control of the system now," he explained, "because I've been there so long, so I can use it to show you behind the scenes at how the group really works."

Eva felt an intense curiosity, as if his decision to move out might unravel a secret clue to the puzzle of her own experience, or to that of Pearl.

"Can we do it with three of us?" Moana came and sat on the arm of the couch beside Eva, resting her hand on Eva's shoulder.

Matt nodded. "I think so."

Eva rubbed Moana's thigh, and, noticing that Matt looked unsettled by their physical intimacy, she teased his neck and hair with the fingers of her other hand to reassure him.

"Why is it forbidden?" Moana asked.

He smiled uncertainly. "They say that it can encourage deep bonds between the participants."

Eva grinned. Just what they didn't need, she thought. However, at the same time, she felt the lure of the technology, and the promise of secrets revealed, like a helpless fascination.

"I think what happens is that you develop a more intuitive contact with one another because you're directing the virtual construct together," he explained, and he laughed. "But calling that dangerous, is a bit like saying that playing football is dangerous because of the communication you develop with your team members."

He smiled, waiting for their response, but they both continued to look at him without saying anything. "I suspect that the leader is trying to break the bonds between members," he explained, "and they've discovered that the link works against this process." He screwed up his face. "But I know the system is capable of link dreaming because of the Way Station capability."

Eva wanted him to change the subject, but Moana was encouraging him by the intensity of her attention.

"If there is a danger with link-dreaming, its the question of who's in control." His eyes lit up. "But I've discovered that the system has an in-built 'Way Station facility', to provide a platform for the communication between multiple dreamers, while they're dreaming."

Moana had an obscene look of curiosity on her face, and Eva realised how much the deep sense of hurt from her split with Pearl was still motivating her.

"Let's do it," she said, grinning mischievously. "I'll get some clothes on." They laughed at her impulsiveness, as she sprang up and went to run upstairs.

"We have to wait a few hours, anyway!" Matt called after her, and there was an edge in his voice which revealed that he hadn't expected to be taken seriously. "We'll have to do it when everyone's asleep."

Moana paused in mid step, looked back at them, shrugged, and continued on. In the background an image was dancing soundlessly on the television.

Eva's fingers were still teasing Matt's neck. She turned to face him, and he leaned slowly towards her. Their lips finally met, and she lost herself in the physical sensations.

"I wanted to tell you this afternoon," he said, "but there wasn't an opportunity." He was wired, and talkative.

She buried her face in his neck. His body smelt sweet. "How come you haven't talked about it before?" she asked.

"I couldn't explain myself." He shook his head. He seemed to drag the answer out of himself. "I couldn't even think. I just had to play along." She felt a shudder run through his body, and she thought of the 'insurance policy' which they had placed under the mattress. It was worse than she could have imagined.

She wanted to know how it really worked, but couldn't formulate a satisfactory question.

"It's like any organism," he said, as if sensing her thoughts. "The urge for survival sometimes compels them to take extreme actions to protect their existence." He turned to face her, and in his eyes she saw the pressures surging below the surface. "That's why I couldn't say anything earlier in front of Pearl, or on the phone."

She nodded.

He seemed to drift away into limbo, like a computer with an overloaded memory. "I still can't really explain it, " he said, coming back to reality. "That's why it would be easier to show you."

She grimaced. She had no desire to get out of bed now that she was warm and relaxed. "When will you move out?" she asked, to change the subject.

"As far as I'm concerned, I've left already."

It was never as easy as that though, she knew. "But where will you stay?"

"I hoped with you."

His pleading eyes left little room for refusal, and she suddenly realised that he imagined himself moving in tonight, and the shock of it made her laugh.

"I don't think I'm quite ready for a live-in lover yet," she told him. "You must have other friends you could stay with."

He shook his head. "Group members are encouraged to break their ties with friends outside the group."

"I guess you might be able to have Pearl's room," she thought out loud. They needed to get someone in, to help with the rent, but the thought of Pearl led her to think of the Awards. "But we really need you there in the group, for the next few days, to help Pearl do her thing with us."

Again he seemed to loose himself as he considered the idea, and she watched emotions of fear and anger rising in his face. Then he nodded reluctantly. "I guess I could stay a few more days."

She was conscious of the pant of his breathing close to her right ear, and the moist sensation of his lips on her neck.

She pulled back and looked in his eyes. Their contact seemed to swim in and out of focus. There were moments of intimacy, and moments of shyness.

The street light outside was throwing shadows from a tree onto the bed. She studied the texture of his skin as he achieved orgasm, watching the ripple of relief in the light down of hair on the back of his neck. And then he collapsed panting on top of her, and she hugged him to her.

They rolled over onto their side, and he rested his head on the pillow. They looked at one another, and he laughed, a little embarrassed at the intimacy, after the compulsive passion of the sex.

She kissed him lightly on the lips, to let him know it was okay. Out the window the faint glow of the new moon was visible.

Moana appeared suddenly at the bedroom door, her leather jacket on, and a determined look on her face.

"Let's move," she said, and Eva felt Matt's body stiffen in response.

Perhaps ungraciously, she found herself wondering how much Moana was motivated by a desire to disturb their intimacy, and how much by her curiosity about the group.

"This is a good time to do it," Matt agreed, "while everyone is asleep or dreaming."

Eva made no move. She did feel more relaxed and at peace than she had for a long time, and so it seemed to pose no threat.

"So, are we going to do it?" Moana asked.

Matt felt like he couldn't back out now, and he scrambled out of bed, and pulled on his clothes.

For a moment Eva considered letting them go by themselves, and then thought better of it, and followed his lead.

22
Virtual Secrets

Eva's heart was beating nervously at the possibility of being discovered, but Matt was moving confidently through the half-darkness of the virtual studio, and she released herself to his care, clinging onto his hand with one of hers, and to Moana's with the other.

She began to sense that a new her was starting to emerge, a self who would do things that she previously would not have done, and she felt a funny sense of security from this encounter with her own growth.

Small grunts, mumbled words, and stirring sounds, were coming from the cubicles around the walls. The muffled noises seemed to recreate the bustle in the city outside; each person absorbed in their own experience, and yet together creating a rich sensual tapestry.

They found an empty cubical, and Matt closed the

curtain quietly behind them. He crossed to the bench, and sat straddling one end, with a leg hanging down either side, and motioned them to sit in front of him.

Eva followed his example, but Moana hung back.

"Maybe I'll stand guard, while you guys do it," she said.

Eva grinned, despite her sense of apprehension. "You wanted to come," she told her, and she pulled Moana's arm playfully to emphasise her comment.

"I just thought someone maybe should stay on guard," Moana mumbled.

Eva relaxed back against Matt's chest, and enjoyed the comfort of their physical contact.

"It will be fine," he assured Moana. "No one checks in here at night." And, unable to resist the direct challenge, she finally straddled the bench and sat in front of Eva.

"Everything okay?" he whispered.

They nodded, and Eva felt the cushion of Moana's hair bounce in front of her.

"Remember I told you about the Way Station?" he asked and again was answered by the bouncing cushion. "We'll go there first," he explained. "Place just your fingertips into the terminals, so we can all get contact."

Eva followed his lead, and there was a brief, and comforting, sensation of settling down to sleep.

She found herself standing with the others in a comfortably furnished room, with large windows which looked out over Kings Cross to the city.

"This is the Way Station," Matt told them.

He seemed to address them directly, but it was more like they could read his thoughts, for his lips didn't move.

"Just think of this room, if you want to talk about anything that's happening while we're dreaming."

"Is this a real room?" Moana asked. She looked already unsettled by the experience.

He shook his head. "It's programmed to resemble one of our rooms, so we feel comfortable here."

Indeed, it was as if they were on the roof of the dream-group's building, Eva thought, and she found that she did feel comfortable, and was beginning to enjoy the sense of adventure she was experiencing. It was much better doing this with her friends, she thought, than by herself.

"I think I'll show you a few things that you already know, to start with," he told them, "and then I'll show you another side of these same events."

Eva had no time to understand what he meant, before she found herself back in a scene in the initiation room. The illusion was much clearer that any of her previous virtual experiences, and this, coupled with the suddenness, sent her a little into shock.

In the next moment, she recognised Pearl as the initiate, and then felt horror as she experienced herself step up, to encounter the document on the table.

Moana had a puzzled look on her face, which pulled Eva out of the trance. Moana hadn't been at the initiation, and her presence now reminded Eva that this was a virtual experience, not a real one, and she felt suddenly lighter for this knowledge.

"I'd like some more information on this, before I sign it," she said, bracing herself against the wind, and she saw Moana nod approvingly.

Matt motioned to the place she should sign, but winked at the same time to reassure her.

She started anticipating the moment when she slipped the copy of the contract down her shirt, and began to dread her subterfuge being revealed to him.

Some instinct told her to clear her mind of any hint of the episode however, and by releasing herself to the experience, she found she was able to ride the flow gently past that moment, without it being revealed. Matt was mainly guiding the dream, and he had no knowledge of the incident so it simply wasn't replayed, and this gave her a wonderful sense of relief.

Then, as the moment approached where she recalled the leader blowing gently, and her falling back, the virtual construct instead had her signing the documents without the falling experience.

This confused her, and she felt the need to ask Matt about it. She looked at him, and as the need to understand grew stronger, the initiation faded about them, and they were back in the room he had called the Way Station.

She was still formulating the question in her mind, when he answered it.

"The system is editing the construct," he told her. Again it was like she could read his thoughts.

"To do what?" she asked.

"To encourage tendencies beneficial to the group."

"And discourage others?"

He nodded.

"Sounds like brain-washing," Moana said. The line of her lips suggested a firmly disapproving attitude.

He shrugged. "Of course it is," he agreed. "But we can change the construct too," he added, "so we have to remember that it's not objective reality here, but more like a dream."

Eva nodded.

Matt waited for each of them to acknowledge his eye contact, and then, with a small flick of his eyes, motioned them on into the experience.

The new scene was in the leader's study. There was a press of group members gathered around the leader, as she sat on one couch, facing Pearl on the other. All around them crowded a sea of faces; crouched close to the floor, peering round the ends of the couches, and standing at the back on chairs. Eva, Matt and Moana stood unnoticed on the fringe of the crowd.

"Not only has Pearl has joined us today," the leader announced, "but she's brought with her young Eva, who stands to receive a good sum of money on her next birthday."

Eva felt a shock at the discovery that their designs on her inheritance were so overt.

"As you know," the leader explained, "we badly need resources for our country retreat in the Blue Mountains." And there was a general nodding and grunting of approval.

She found Pearl's reaction the most worrying, however, because she didn't seem at all surprised at the news. And as the hands behind the faces started to applaud her, she even broke into a broad grin.

They were suddenly back in the Way Station, and Eva flopped into one of the chairs, and waited for her thoughts to settle.

Moana stood shaking her head, her hair brushing the

air from side to side. "She can be a selfish bastard, but that seems unreal." Again it was like they could sense one another's thoughts.

Although Eva guessed, on replaying the scene in her mind, that Pearl was probably forced into playing that role by the circumstances, she still felt betrayed by her friend. Particularly when she thought about all the effort she had gone to maintain their contact, and she reacted by rejecting her, and releasing her to her fate.

Moana looked quite worried, and Eva took her hand. Slowly her friend's expression developed a look of resolution, and this resolve seemed to carry them off again on their roller coaster ride.

The leader cleared her throat. She was standing right in front of the crazy woman from one of those first evenings, standing right in her line of vision, but there was no sign of response on the woman's face. She just sat and stared with a belligerent look, her cheaply made dress sitting awkwardly on her thin shoulders.

The construct was rough and rowdy, the gathering more like a rabble than anything Matt would create, and Eva knew she wasn't dreaming it, so she figured Moana must be finding her feet on the system.

The scene jumped forward to the stand-off with the guards. For another long moment they stood there. The leader playing with them like a cat with an insect. Eva felt an underlying horror to the stand-off, which because of the excitement of the original gathering she had not been aware of at the time.

"The crazy one can go," the leader said. The security line parted, and slowly the woman detached herself from Moana, and was about to be sucked out through the door, when again the construct dissolved into another scene in the study.

Matt, the leader, and three or four other prominent group members were there. And although Eva and Moana were standing right behind Matt, nobody appeared to notice them.

"That Kiwi woman played right into your hands tonight," someone told the leader. It wasn't clear who was speaking.

"We definitely need to break Pearl's bond with this person," the leader advised them.

"That's the third time that crazy woman has been here," someone else told the leader.

She nodded. "That's why I was so hard on her. I don't think she'll come back again."

They smiled and shook their heads.

"Sometimes people don't hear messages unless they are strongly expressed," she said. "And it provided a good opportunity to demonstrate the value of a clear authority."

There were nods and murmurs of approval.

Eva found herself back in the room overlooking the Cross.

"She's simply demonstrating to Pearl that she is stronger than you," Matt whispered to Moana. "That whatever individual freedom you have, it's only at her discretion."

"I see," Moana murmured. "That's not what I wanted."

"Do you want to go on?" he asked.

"I want to know why you're moving out."

Eva nodded. That's why they were here.

Matt looked a little embarrassed, and his lips compressed into a fine line, and this tone seemed to flip the scene back again to the leader's study. He seemed to be working hard to create this experience, possible against some resistance from the machine.

"That Kiwi woman played right into your hands tonight." It was Matt speaking these words.

"We definitely need to break Pearl's bond with this person," the leader advised them.

Eva grimaced with embarrassment at his two faced behaviour, and Moana bit her lip as she realised how she had been manipulated.

"We've really got to be careful of Pearl's tendency to bond with such people," the leader told Matt. "You can see from her chart printout that this tendency is her soft underbelly. We just have to make sure she bonds with us, and not outsiders."

"Is there any Pluto activity coming up?" Matt asked her.

The leader looked at the printout for some moments, then nodded. "If we do some intensive feedback in a month's time, we should be able to establish new patterns which are healthier for her stay in the group."

They smiled.

"And you seem to be making good progress with her friend Eva," she told him.

"She is becoming besotted with me," he said, obviously using the terms she wanted.

Eva felt a deep disquiet at hearing him say this, but she realised that he was making himself vulnerable by exposing his part in the manipulation and, appreciating the candour of his confession, she forgave him.

"Just so long as you don't become besotted with her," the leader told him.

Matt shook his head, but Eva felt him take her hand behind his back, and press it in contradiction of the dream image. This contradiction seemed to throw a wobble into the experience, and it slowly dissolved around them.

The air was heavy and dark, and Eva wasn't sure where they were. A large metal door swung suddenly open before them, and they walked down a corridor with what looked like cell doors on either side. Eva couldn't bring herself to look through the grills on any of the doors, but she had the sickening sense that human rights had no value within these walls.

Through the open door at the end of the corridor she heard the leader's voice raised in anger, followed by a cry of pain.

Fear grew in her chest, and she stopped.

Beads of sweat stood on Matt's brow, as the scene dissolved.

There was a jarring blackness, which awoke her suddenly back to the awareness of the virtual cubicle. A light was flashing, and in the distance an alarm was sounding quietly, changing tone every few moments, like a car alarm.

To her horror she discovered the leader and two guards confronting them with weapons. The atmosphere was alive with intimidation, and for a moment she considered the possibility that it was still a virtual experience. Then she felt pain as the barrel of a gun was jabbed under her ribs, and she turned to face the consequences of their foolish actions.

"I told you I should have stood guard," Moana hissed.

Eva took her hand. "What would you have done?"

She shrugged.

"I'm very disappointed in you," the leader hissed at Matt. "Very, very disappointed." She was standing directly in front of him, staring down into his face. Fear grabbed at Eva's throat as she felt the raw hatred in her voice.

"That's all right," he responded calmly, "I grew disappointed with you some time ago."

She slapped him hard, and the act of violence echoed through the room.

Eva's fear intensified with this confirmation they were at the mercy of someone who wielded absolute power within these walls. Her heart was pounding like a drum.

Matt, however, made no response, and, after a moment, it began to feel like the leader had gone too far, too soon. He had provoked her to reveal her true colours before she was ready and, to cover this, she changed her approach.

"The newcomers can go," she instructed the guards. She motioned to Matt. "I want to see him in my study in five minutes." And she walked out.

Eva found she could breath again, but her heart was still racing. She didn't want to leave Matt here.

"You don't have to stay," Moana echoed her thoughts.

"We'll all go together," she told the guards.

Eva squeezed her hand. Moana's bold statement was belied however by the weapons in the guard's hands, and their silent intimidating stares. She had grown pretty close to Moana over the past few weeks, and she felt her restrain herself, apparently learning that her natural impulses might work against her best interests.

"It's okay," Matt reassured them both. "Remember, I have my insurance."

Eva felt a flood of relief. Suddenly she understood how important it was to him, that they were released.

Moana also smiled, at this immediate verification of her new restraint.

"Let's just get out of here," Eva told her. She was cursing herself for jeopardising the fragile deal over Pearl that they had struck yesterday, and torn between leaving Matt, and the urgent need to pick up the envelope from under her mattress.

Through all this however, Matt was sitting calmly. She guessed he was glad it had come to a head.

She wanted to lean toward him and seek reassurance in his lips, but she felt too intimidated by the weapons. She turned to go, and felt her heart wrench with fear at this new turn of events.

23

Rehearsal

Dawn was creeping across the sky, and for a few long minutes there were no cabs through the Cross. Eva and Moana half ran down the street, picking their way over people asleep in doorways, and past prostitutes standing casually in the cold early hours. There were still a few late night revellers around, but without the wash of the crowds, the Cross looked very seedy.

"They'll be after us, as soon as Matt tells them about the list," Eva said, voicing her fears in an effort to clear her mind of the numbness she was feeling, and she heard the words ring amidst their footfalls. Moana made no answer, and Eva looked at her and found her face glowing with excitement.

"Whoa!" she exclaimed, "That was something huh?" Her eyes were wide, and slightly wild.

Eva simply nodded. It was going to take her time to process the experience, and for now her fear for Matt, and her sense of guilt for her part in the debacle, wouldn't let her focus on anything but their immediate escape.

"He won't tell them that we've got it," she said, "but they'll work it out."

A taxi cruised around the corner, and she urgently flagged it down. It felt like the danger had given her a clarity of insight about what to do. "We'll pick up the list, and go straight on to Angel's," she decided, as the car drew to a halt beside them.

"At this hour of the morning?" Moana chuckled. She opened the back door of the taxi. "We'll be waking her up." She climbed into the car.

Eva shrugged. She couldn't understand her attitude. Waking Angel was the least of her worries. Her heart was beating wildly.

She raced into the house to get the list, and as she negotiated the front door, the living room, and the stairs, she was conscious only of the physical sensations of her body, and of the incredibly slow pace of each moment.

Her hand groped under the mattress and found the precious piece of paper, and instantly she breathed easier. Her eyes fell on the ruffled bed sheets, and for a moment she allowed herself to feel the happiness and warmth she had shared there with Matt just a few hours before.

Tears appeared in the corner of her eyes at the mess they seemed to have made of it, and she blinked them away as she went back downstairs.

She leapt with relief back into the car, and took Moana's outstretched hand, seeking comfort in their contact. She allowed the acceleration of the car to push her gently back into the seat, and a shiver ran down her spine.

As they pulled out of the street, they passed a car going the other way with 'Dare to Dream' painted on the side, and she instinctively pulled Moana out of sight, as it passed.

"Are you crazy?" Moana asked irritably.

"I recognised the car."

She snorted. "Soon you'll be seeing helicopters, and missiles."

Eva caught a glimpse of the driver's eyes in the rear vision mirror, and saw a reflection of the two wild women in his early-morning cab. She started giggling a little hysterically, and this just compounded the image in his eyes.

They did wake Angel, but Eva was so glad to hear the bolt of the lock clicking into place on the door behind them that she thought nothing of it.

The curtains were pulled, cocooning the apartment from the expanse of city outside, and she allowed herself to relax for the first time since struggling out of the dream. She found her legs starting to shake, and realised she felt sick in her stomach. She half staggered over to the table, tossed the list onto it, and collapsed in one of the chairs.

Moana followed her lead, and sat down. She was still buzzing from the experience.

Angel stood looking at them. She wasn't angry, but her face told them that it had to be important to wake her early on the morning of the dress rehearsal, and she was waiting for answers.

"This is a file of investment data controlled by the group leader," Eva told her, motioning to the sheet of paper. "Matt swears that she will do anything to stop this information being revealed."

Angel looked from one to the other of them. "Tell me the rest of this story," she invited them, and Eva left it to Moana to recount the story of Matt's late night arrival, and their subsequent adventures.

Angel's face wore an amused smile through most of the tale, and it was only when Moana got to the weapons, that Angel realised how serious it really was, and that they had jeopardised everything with their hair-brained midnight prank, that she grew really angry.

"How could you be so stupid?" she spat at them.

The comment echoed Eva's own judgement of herself, but nevertheless she bristled at her attack. "We've got little green men with machine guns chasing us around in taxis," she told her, "we don't need you hassling us as well."

Angel glared at her.

Eva had never seen her this way before, and the confrontation increased the gnawing sensation in her stomach. "I just keep thinking of Matt trapped in there," she said, and she felt little beads of tears forming again in the corner of her eyes, which she did her best to blink away.

Angel sensed from her tone that there was more to her relationship with Matt, and she looked at Moana for explanation.

Moana nodded, and made a ring shape with the fingers of one hand, and a fucking gesture with the other, and they all laughed at the simple vulgarity of it, and this seemed to break the feeling of emotional impasse in the room.

Angel picked up the sheet of paper, and, after a moments study, she whistled. "This is hot," she said. Her eyes were wide. "We'll just threaten to send this to the media," she crowed, "and give them a deadline."

Eva nodded. That's what she had been trying to say, but somehow it still felt like a desperate last attempt.

She felt exhausted, and lay down in Angel's room, while the boss plotted strategy with Moana, and hassled on the phone with the lawyers. She wanted to sleep, but at first her mind was restless, and the uncomfortable sensation in her guts wouldn't let her settle down.

Somewhere nearby, a jackhammer started pounding. It wasn't the noise so much that grated on Eva, but rather the way it seemed to vibrate through the fabric of the building, and then through her bones.

After a time, she began to feel hot and feverish, and she started tossing and turning in the bed. She discovered a tickle in her throat, and began to worry that she was really getting ill. The fear that, even if it all came together for the Awards, she might be unable to participate, gnawed further at her attempts to settle down. It seemed the ultimate irony, and made her just want to give up trying altogether.

This release eventually helped her to drop off, but still she slept only fitfully. As well as dealing with her physical sensations, and her emotions, she was still processing the virtual experience, and images from those events kept recurring in her dreams.

The day dragged on, and the snatches of sleep, and slow unwinding of her thoughts, gradually refreshed Eva. When she finally awoke without the fever shakes, it was well into the afternoon, and the phone was ringing insistently in the next room. She couldn't understand why no-one was answering it, and then it stopped, and there was silence.

She lay still, and allowed the sensations of the afternoon. She felt much stronger, but she still had a little tickle in her throat, and tight ball of worry in her guts, and she tried not to think of Matt, or what he might be going through, because that just made it worse.

The phone rang again, and she considered getting up to answer it herself, but her thoughts were still moving so slowly, that she had come to no conclusion, by the time she heard the toilet flushing, and finally Angel answered the machine.

Eva's gaze was caught by the light from an array of crystals on the window sill. Angel's bedroom was cluttered with little bits and pieces on every surface, and there were piles of clothes scattered across the floor. The room had the feeling of an animal's lair, quite the opposite of her sophisticated outside demeanour.

The phone conversation in the next room suddenly increased in volume. "... at Circular Quay," Eva heard Angel demand, "in an hour." There was a pause, then

Eva heard her slam down the receiver and give a whoop of delight.

Her head appeared around the door. "I need you to run an errand," she said. "Are you up to it?"

Eva nodded, wondering what it was.

"I've arranged for you to meet your boyfriend, and get a written commitment from them," she said, and, without further explanation, she disappeared.

Eva's heart leapt, and she scrambled quickly out of bed. She couldn't believe it was true, but still she ran into the bathroom, to throw cold water on her face and freshen up.

She found him leaning against the harbour rail at Circular Quay. Two men were conspicuously watching from a short distance away, and the vibe of intimidation somewhat over-shadowed her huge sense of relief at their meeting.

"Did they hurt you?" she asked him tenderly, noticing that there were marks on his face.

"This is just from that slap," he said fingering the bruises.

There was a faint smell of diesel fumes from the ferries, mixed with the smell of salt, and the air was alive with the cry's of seagulls. She felt a funny sense of lightness, as if the bump and grind of the world about them, was more like a film, or a stage set.

"Are they here so you don't run away?" she asked, motioning to the guards.

He nodded. "I've been grounded."

"What's that?"

"I'm confined to my room, with no outside contact."

"But you're here now?" She still couldn't really believe it, and she touched his arm to reassure herself.

"Your lawyer's threats have bent the rules," he explained.

She leaned over and kissed him. His lips were definitely real, and she felt a surge of energy from the contact, however out of the corner of her eye, she saw the guards take a few steps closer.

"What's to stop us just running away?" she asked. "They'd never catch us."

He shook his head. "I'll play along till the Awards tomorrow."

She nodded, and yet it seemed too uncertain, and possibly better to take their chance now, while they still could. "What about Pearl?" She still felt hurt and rejected by Pearl's behaviour, and this showed in the tone of her voice.

By way of answer, Matt handed her an envelope, and she slipped it down her shirt.

"Sometimes we do things that are more a product of the circumstances, than our own intentions," he told her, sensing her feelings.

"Is she okay?"

"More than okay." A small smile played on his lips. "We had a good to talk this afternoon."

She felt mixed emotions at the news. "I thought you said you'd had no contact?"

"She was checking me out for the leader," he winked.

She nodded. "How do you mean, more than okay?"

"Now she's being honoured by the group for participating in the Awards."

It didn't seem to make any sense, and just added to her bewilderment about what was really happening for Pearl, and how to respond to it.

"It's a new strategy," he explained. "The leader's giving her lots of credit for honouring the group in this way."

It changed on a whim, she thought, but still it sounded more positive, and her spirits lifted a little. He was gazing into the distance after a departing ferry, and she watched the little movements of his eyes, as his thoughts ticked over.

"It would be good if you could come to the Awards tomorrow?" she told him.

"Maybe I can, if you request it." He turned back to her. They were standing very close, so that she could feel his breath on her cheek, and after a moment their lips touched. The guards edged a little closer. "That could be a good opportunity to make a break," he whispered.

She pulled back, and looked at him. The proposal both worried and excited her. "But, there's also the security at the Entertainment Centre to think about."

His eyes lit up. "That's the answer. If I make a run for the stage, the venue security would remove me, and keep the group's guards away."

It sounded risky, and she found herself biting her lip. "Maybe if we can get them to help us," she suggested, and she kicked herself for even allowing the possibility of such a hair-brained scheme.

She found the stage door at the Entertainment Centre, and stood confronting the security attendants. It was as if they didn't even know that there was a rehearsal on tonight, or maybe they were just playing with her, she didn't really know.

She considered broaching the stunt idea with them, but thought better of it. The didn't look co-operative, and she decided it would be better to talk directly to the stage security at tomorrow night's performance.

As she walked down the bare corridor, she encountered someone coming out of one of the other dressing rooms, and recognised her as the lead singer with a woman's heavy-rock band. She smiled in greeting as they passed one another.

"Good luck newcomer," the woman called as she disappeared, the hiss in her tone however giving the lie to her words.

Eva shivered as she walked on, checking the name on each door, until she came to one labelled, 'Dance Sisters'.

Pearl was there already, and they stood looking at one another for a long moment. Then she broke into a little quick-step, which was one of their signature movements, and despite the shadow of betrayal, it suddenly felt like old times, as Eva fell into step with her

"How come you're so happy?" Eva asked.

"Things just seem to be going my way."

"Are you getting support at home for this now?"

Pearl nodded.

Eva bit her lip. She wanted to shout, 'Don't you see! Don't you see how you're being manipulated by them!'. But she was determined not to disturb the fragile truce before tomorrow's Awards.

Pearl smiled. "I know about your link stuff," she said, sensing what Eva was feeling. "It's hardly surprising you feel the way you do. If you link with a drop-out, he'll show you the drop-out's perspective."

Eva let it ride. She felt purged of expectations by the chaotic events of the past few weeks, and it was enough for her that Pearl was here for the work.

Moana burst in, leaving the door to swing closed by itself behind her. She held a frangipani flower in each hand, and there was one in her hair.

She walked up to Pearl, stood eyeballing her for some moments, then offered her a flower. Eva sensed in the gesture the twin bond of love and antagonism between them. "Sorry for blaming you," she said, with a slight quiver in her voice.

Pearl stood bemused. The white and yellow tinge of the bloom in her hand, sang against the dull concrete block wall of the room. "Blaming me for?"

"Fucking us up," Moana said, "for your own selfish pleasure."

Pearl nodded thoughtfully. "And now you know that ..." She left the sentence hanging as an invitation.

"You're just a victim of their games." Moana finished it.

Pearl grinned at her former lover's attempt to excuse her behaviour, and Eva sensed Moana's confidence cracking slightly under the steady stare.

"I'm doing what I'm doing because I want to," Pearl told them.

Eva felt a choking sensation in her throat. "After all the work you've put into the Dance Sisters," she couldn't help but remind her, "to suddenly pull back like you have been?"

"We all know that I've had problems with Angel," Pearl admitted. "And I've been working through this stuff in the Processing Sessions."

Eva wished she hadn't said it.

"What I've discovered," Pearl went on, "is a need for transformative experiences, underneath the need for attention, which drives me to perform."

Eva could see the attitudes of the group underpinning this interpretation, and she felt a whiff of the fear she had felt there last night.

"And I'm just more able to fulfil this in the group," Pearl told them, "than I am in the current line-up of the Dance Sisters."

Eva knew she had to respect Pearl's feelings, even though she couldn't agree with her, and this made her keenly aware of the separation between their lives, and of the effort they all had to make to work together. She kissed her impulsively on the cheek, and was reassured by their sudden intimacy.

Moana offered Eva the other flower, and she lifted it to her nose and smelt the delicate fragrance, so light and yet so strong. She kissed Moana, and caught again the frangipani smell from the flower in her friend's hair.

Beyond the curtains the auditorium was empty and cavernous, without the audience, and yet at the same time somehow full of expectations, which were wafted about by the heat from the spot-lights, and the "Check, one, two," from the sound technicians.

They stood in the wings of the stage, waiting for their rehearsal slot. For the first time, Eva really felt the challenge of the competition tomorrow night. Until now all her focus had been on getting to this point, and now the scale of the undertaking made her feel very small in comparison.

"These guy's are a bit much," Pearl grumbled, motioning to the act on stage. It was the band with the singer who had hissed at Eva in the corridor. They were well over time with their sound check, and were still fussing with the levels of their instruments. Pearl stepped onto the stage, caught the singer's eye, and gave her a signal to wind it up.

The woman aggressively gestured with her index finger, and then, with a brief command to the rest of the band, they launched into their particular brand of upbeat heavy-pop.

As soon as the woman's band had finished, the Dance

Sisters marched onto stage, without waiting for the others to pack off the equipment.

"I hear you guys can't get it up for one another any more?" Eva overheard the singer call to Pearl. She was laughing at her own supposed joke.

Pearl ignored her as she continued to pace out her steps and get a feel for the space as best she could.

"Pity," the singer said, as she turned to go, "cause that's about all you had going for you." The raw competitive vibe grated in her voice.

Moana turned and gestured playfully after her as if to punch her, only allowing Pearl and Eva to restrain her with seeming difficulty.

Eva was glad to see that they still had a playful energy together, and the personal nature of the attack seemed to bring them closer together. The interaction actually provided a welcome release as they began their sound check.

It was as she heard their voices ring out through the empty auditorium, however, that she began to feel comfortable in the team once again. She was a small part of the experience, but together they wove a pattern which was larger, infinitely more rich and varied.

The demands of the dancing always got her heart going, and she enjoyed the surge of energy about her body. There was a slight pressure in her head, and she relaxed her breathing, and felt the pressure clear.

As she accepted the present moment, she found a new depth of emotion reflected in the quality of the tones of her voice. She caught Moana's eye, and a big grin broke out on each of their faces as they savoured the excitement of the Awards tomorrow night.

She slept fitfully that night, waking every now and then at sudden noises from the world outside. She was half expecting a commando raid to materialise from behind the curtains and snatch away the precious chance that was again almost within their reach, and she snuggled down under the covers in the absurd, but comforting, belief that this kept her safe from evil.

Sometime in the early morning, Moana crept into bed with her, and the warmth of their bodies comforted one another again. Somewhere in the sensations of moisture on their breath, the involuntary twitching of muscles, and the rhythmic beat of their hearts, Eva found a connection with a life force that felt strong and immediate, and could refresh her, even in the face of the chaos in her life, and this discovery allowed her to finally relax into a deep sleep.

24

Song Awards

Eva slept well into the middle of the day, and Moana was long up and out, by the time she finally arose. She found herself floating about the house with an unreal sense of grace. She kept expecting some drama to interrupt the quiet flow of each moment, but all the appliances worked as usual, and there were no sudden emergencies in the street outside.

She took a cup of tea out into the garden, and spent time warming-up her voice. She allowed the notes to sound out through the bamboo, playing lightly with them, and felt the pressure from the world beyond.

Amidst the chaos of forces acting upon the planet, and the thrash of change in their personal lives, their familiar little space felt like a paper cut out, against the busy collage of life.

Pearl came unexpected over in the middle of the day, and found her still in the garden. Pearl seemed calm and at peace with herself, and her presence firmed up the paper cut out and made it real.

"You were just passing?" Eva asked. She felt slightly on guard, so as not to let on about her plan with Matt.

"I brought you a book," Pearl responded, pulling a small, brightly coloured paperback out of her pocket.

Astrology Now, declared the bold letters on the cover. Eva turned it over to read the blurb on the back.

"This book represents the insight of ten years of research into the relationship between social interaction, and astrological birth tendencies, at the Dream-group in Kings Cross."

She found herself reacting against what she sensed was conditioning from the group, but was also intrigued by the insight it might lend.

"Because of the nature of the living situation, and the intimate participation of each group member, the research has been detailed, and the results and theories espoused are firmly based in the experiential data."

She slipped the book into the pocket of her cotton jacket which hung on the back of the chair.

Pearl was sitting quietly, allowing the flow of the passing moments, and her face seemed to glow with a white aura.

"I'm glad you came over," Eva admitted. "I've been feeling a little spaced out here by myself."

Pearl nodded. "I'm glad I don't have that problem any more." She grinned.

She seemed so full of life that Eva felt jealous of her new lifestyle. And suddenly her sense of bewilderment about Pearl's motives, dissolved into a new sense of understanding, a realisation that, in undertaking these challenges, Pearl was honouring a need in her soul, to grow. And in honouring her own need to grow, she was also catalysing a regeneration in Eva.

Eva felt light-headed from this insight into the karmic dance of their relationship, an insight which overcame the petty jealousies and betrayals of the mundane reality. She felt warm toward Pearl again, in a way in which she had closed herself off from in recent days, and she leaned over and kissed her.

Moana returned, her overalls splattered with paint, and her face beaming and relaxed from the pleasure of decorating their truck for the parade.

Eva reached out and touched her fingers in greeting.

"Coming to the Mardigras party tonight after the Awards?" Moana asked Pearl.

Pearl shook her head. "Don't have a ticket." Her eyes

were on their hand contact, trying to read the change in their relationship. "I hear they're up to five hundred on the black market."

Moana grinned. "I bet I could get you in."

"Are you inviting me out?" Pearl asked, and her feet moved restlessly at the thought.

Moana shook her head. "Definitely not." The idea seemed to sober her momentarily.

"Are you meeting us at the Entertainment Centre, after the parade?" Eva asked Moana. She was trying to work out how she was going to fit in the Song Awards, with all her other activities.

Moana nodded. "And then off to the party."

"Just popping in, between your other gigs?" Pearl asked her, a little sarcastically. The rub was still there between them.

"You can talk," Moana responded. "I've checked it all out with Angel." She released Eva's hand and, reaching over, tousled Pearl's hair as if she were a child. "It's planned down to the minute."

Eva felt her heart catch in her throat, as she anticipated Pearl's reaction to this patronising gesture. Their hopes still felt so fragile, that a small gesture such as this, could destroy everything, but Pearl thankfully didn't bite.

Eva walked alone to the gig that night, and enjoyed the solitude, the bustle of the city around her, the glimpses of the stars through the city lights, and the regular release of energy in the footfalls of her feet.

The city was pulsing. Already Oxford Street was closed in preparation for the Gay and Lesbian Mardigras Parade, and all the surrounding streets were alive with people. Many were carrying plastic milk crates to stand on, so as to get a good view over the crowd when it started. Others had already taken up their position, and the excitement level was building with the imminent start of the event.

As she arrived at the Entertainment Centre, she paused in front of a poster for the Awards. The bright faces of last year's winners, stared out at her. There were three of them, and for a moment it seemed as if it were the Dance Sister's faces on next year's poster, and the image buoyed her spirits as she entered the building.

She found Angel in the Green Room, with the other agents, journalists, notables and their hangers on. She was chatting with a journalist, and gesturing expansively with her wine glass.

Eva reflected on her value to the trio, as she waited to catch her attention. She dared to believe in her own wild schemes, and because of her faith, was able to realise them. She was also good at the social games, which was so important in this business. In contrast Eva felt uncomfortable amidst the dance of puffed up egos in the room, and she noticed that few of the other performers were there.

"Where are the others?" she asked Angel, as the journalist mingled on across the room,

"You're the first here." Angel sounded a little drunk. She pulled a performer's pass out of her pocket, and handed it to her. Then she bent forward to kiss her on the cheek. "Good luck," she whispered. "I've done as much as I can. It's up to you guys now."

Eva nodded. Half of her mind was working on how to get the security guards to co-operate with Matt's escape, so she didn't really register the added pressure implied in the comment. She pinned the pass to her collar.

Screwing up her resolve, she stole down the stairs at the side of the stage, then walked up the narrow passage between the crowd barrier and the side of the stage platform. The venue was packed already. The wash of noise from the audience engulfed her, and she felt awed by the mass energy of the crowd.

As she turned the corner at the front of the stage, she encountered two security guards. They turned towards her with startled expressions, then made a grab for her, and only stopped when they saw the pass pinned to her collar.

"I'm with the Dance Sisters," she introduced herself, "one of the acts tonight?" They nodded, and relaxed, suddenly beaming with pleasure at meeting her, and she proceeded to confide their plan in them, making it out, as Matt had suggested, to be a stunt which was part of their act.

The two guards from the other side of the stage, intrigued by the disturbance, sauntered over, and stood behind their companions, checking out the excitement. Then they conferred amongst themselves. Eva realised that her heart was pounding in her chest.

She peered round the fly curtain at the side of stage, and drank in the roar of chatter from the huge crowd which had packed the centre to overflowing. Pearl was pacing up and down behind her, because Moana was late, and Eva finally felt the awesome challenge which lay before them.

She spied Matt sitting in one of the reserved seats in the front row, and breathed a sigh of relief at seeing him there, a feeling that was only slightly dampened by the knowledge that the two big guys, sitting on either side of him, were there to defeat his escape plan.

The crowd were in a boisterous mood, and the band

on stage were milking the applause, playing the clown to prolong their time on stage and beat up their chances of winning.

Moana arrived, just as the woman's band were about to start. She was soft and steaming from the cathartic release of playing out her wild nature in the parade, and the three of them embraced at the side of the stage. Their bodies seemed to melt into one another, and an 'oomm' sprang naturally from their vocal chords.

Eva marvelled at how all their personal difficulties disappeared, now that the experience was upon them. It seemed that all their trials on the road to this moment, had simply made them conscious of the process of working together, and their ambition now gave each of them the focus to make it happen.

Against the background of the applause for the previous act, they harmonised their energies, ready for the performance.

Then the experience was upon them. She felt an energy rush, at the roar of the crowd as they entered the stage. They took their positions, and waited a few moments for the backing track to start.

She felt at once hugely powerful, and also extremely

vulnerable to be the focus of so much attention, but as the first notes from their voices strode strongly out into the arena of the theatre, she lost herself in the articulation of the song, and the rhythmic movements of the dance.

Pearl's enjoyment of the movement was contagious, and immediately before the stage a few people caught the enthusiasm, and began dancing in front of their seats.

Eva took care to let her notes play with Moana's, picking up on the energy when the song called for it, and dancing quickly across the expectations of the audience at other times, so as to leave them entranced. She had completely lost her sense of vulnerability, and felt the power of the music surging through her.

As the number progressed, more and more people started dancing, which hadn't happened to any other number so far, and this response fed their performance even more.

The excitement hung like a burst of fireworks in the background, as they took their applause.

Matt suddenly made his run, and with a couple of leaps he was over the crowd barrier before his guards could even react. By the time they jumped after him, two of the security guards had pinned him against the stage, and four others stood preventing the group's heavies from reaching him.

One of the security guards looked at Eva for confirmation he was the right guy. She nodded, and watched them dragging him backstage to their dressing room as she had arranged. The two guards from the Dream-group started arguing with the security men, and more security hurried from the sides of the stage to the scene of the disturbance.

Sitting with all the other performers backstage, and waiting for the judges decision, Eva felt they had a real chance of winning, and the excitement kept bubbling up inside her, but every time it did, her fear of failure kept pushing it down again.

She realised suddenly that her vision had, until now, been focused solely towards the competition itself, and that she hadn't thought where it might lead beyond that. But now she felt the possibility, and the challenge, of representing Australia in Tokyo.

The suspense was deadly as they heard the presenter open the envelope. "And the winner is... the Dance Sisters!"

As their name was called out Moana leapt into the air with a whoop. Pearl and Eva stood, and the three of them walked onto the stage to the thunderous applause of the crowd.

They looked at one another, and, in this heightened reality, she felt an underlying strength, or sense of fate, about their relationship, which seemed to transcend the turmoil of their everyday lives.

They bowed, and, as the protocol required, launched into a 30 second grab of their hit.

She found Matt in the dressing room afterwards, and collapsed into his arms. She felt higher than she had ever felt before, and almost faint from the experience.

"We won!" she told him.

He nodded. "It went well," he agreed, "but your production was boring."

She looked at him. Perhaps it was a joke. She couldn't decide.

Pearl entered, and stood staring at Matt, obviously wary of his intrusion into their backstage space.

Eva realised that his leaving the group must challenge her faith in it, and she stepped back to allow this to be resolved. For a moment it looked like Pearl was going to say something, but then she set about to ignore him.

"The lighting was bland," he continued, ignoring her in turn, "and there was a slight distortion on one of the microphones."

Eva smiled, despite the awkwardness in the room.

Trust him to notice those sort of things, she thought.

"You can do much better, anyway" he told them.

"You sound like you're applying for a job," Pearl barked.

"Maybe I am," he told her. "You'd be lucky to get me." She grinned incredulously.

"It could also be good for you to have someone here," he suggested, "someone who understands what you're going through with the group."

Pearl had to think about this, and Eva realised that his involvement with them might indeed bring more balance to the enterprise, and she took his hand and caressed his fingers.

Pearl however, having appraised him with her look, then grimaced. "I'd be just a little worried by your lack of loyalty," she said with mock seriousness.

"I'm just following my own path," he told her, "like you are." There was a real sense of honesty in his voice. "I don't think bad things about the group, although I feel a little embarrassed by some of the manipulative games in which I participated." He shot a quick glance at Eva. "But I still feel it was a valuable period of my life."

"The games are just the tools for the learning process," Pearl responded quickly, and Eva could see her already mastering some of the necessary 'correct attitudes'.

Eva caught Matt's eye, and they smiled in a knowing,

and, at least somewhat, accepting way.

Angel entered with Moana. Each was carrying a bottle of champagne and some glasses.

"We pulled it off!" Angel congratulated them. "After all the drama, we pulled it off!" She was almost beside herself with excitement, and had lost her normal sense of composure. She started imitating one of their dance routines, and she looked so funny that they all burst into laughter.

Moana set about opening her bottle, and after a moment the cork flew off with a loud pop. She poured some into a glass, and held it up to watch the bubbles against the light.

"To our continued success together," she cheekily proposed a toast, looking directly at Pearl, and the look on Pearl's face said that she also hadn't been thinking beyond tonight, and the prospect of Tokyo now loomed before her.

Eva felt the pull of the excitement of the adventure on Pearl, and at the same time the push of uncertainty about whether she would be allowed to participate.

"This is where my involvement might be helpful," Matt suggested, and Pearl looked at him for some moments, until she eventually acknowledged his support with a slight movement of her eyes.

Oblivious to this, Moana passed Eva the glass of wine, and picked up the bottle to fill some more.

Eva found her hand was shaking, and she set the glass down. Thinking that she felt cold, she reached for her cotton jacket, which was hanging on a clothes hook on the wall. It was probably just the tension release after the show, she told herself, as the softness of the material comforted her.

Angel picked up one of the glasses. "To your brilliant work tonight!" She quickly focused them on their current success.

"And to our tolerance for one another," Eva added, picking up her glass. The shaking had thankfully stilled.

Pearl took the final glass. She looked into it for a moment. "And the freedom to be ourselves," she added.

They each drank, and Eva found the wine fizzed up her nose from the inside. Again she had this sense of fate about their relationship. Somehow there was an order in the destiny of each of them, that threw them together despite the ebb and flow of their individual experiences.

Eva felt something heavy in her pocket, and her fingers found the astrology book that Pearl had given her earlier. She was going to enjoy reading it, she thought.

Moana threw her wine back in one gulp, and put the glass down. "I'm out of here," she said. She flashed each them a grin. "It's time to party."

www.ingramcontent.com/pod-product-compliance
Lightning Source LLC
Chambersburg PA
CBHW060433030726
47495CB00003B/857